The Alibi
and
Other Stories

ISBN: 10:0615648819
ISBN: 13:978-0615648811

Contents: Life, Love, Fire, Fat, and Food... - Clouds' Illusions – The Alibi – The Far End of the Beach – A New Millennium – Does Jesus Save the Living? – Capital G God – White Daisies

Hawk Bluff Publishing
Lenoir City, TN

www.josephmichaeldegross.com

The following stories in this collection originally appeared elsewhere: "Life, Love, Fire, Fat and Food...," *Literary Lunch;* "Clouds' Illusions," *North American Review;* "The Alibi," *The Literary Review;* "The Far End of the Beach," as a chapter in the author's novel, *Undertow,* in slightly different form; "A New Millennium," *Carve Magazine*

For Herman and John

ACKNOWLEDGMENTS

As always, I am grateful to my readers, past and present, including Susan Newell, Mary Bess Dunn, Mary Buckner, Gretchen DeGross-Girgenti, Diana Koga, and Robert Silich for their insight and suggestions. I thank my wife, Sandra, for encouraging my writing. And thanks to Rebecca Brown and Tom Jenks, who helped me find the narrative voice for these stories.

Life is a series of problems.
Happy people are problem-solvers.

JM DeGross, MD

CONTENTS

*LIFE, LOVE, FIRE, FAT
AND FOOD ARE MOSTLY
FOUR-LETTER WORDS*

Martin Stoker sat at the bar in the *Fire in the Hole* tavern. It was a dump; dollar bills stuck up all over the walls, the smell of stale beer, and everything in the place worn and threadbare. It was known, in the local vernacular, as a gin mill. Martin's ass folded over both sides of the barstool like an ameba trying to engulf food. He was six feet and three inches, one end to the other, but if you ran a measuring tape along his front surface, it added two and a half more feet to allow for his huge belly and chest. His neck was lost in chin-folds, and he had plenty of dark-brown curly hair on his head, back, chest, legs and arms. Naked, which was not a pretty sight, he looked like a great ape. His suit size was sixty-two and if you hooked two of his belts together, they could tie-down a twenty-inch sewer pipe on a flatbed trailer.

Like most of us, he was flawed—had problems, this very fat man. Food, it seemed, was one. Martin Stoker needed a constant supply of food: cold food, hot food, raw food, cooked food, ethnic food, plain food, fancy food, seafood, spicy food, good food, bad food, fast food, junk food, vegetables, candy, meat, bread, sugar, fish, fruit, fowl, food high in cholesterol, food high in vitamins—he absolutely, without any reservation, or self-control, needed to eat, and he knew why. His parents. Believing they were doing a good thing, they taught him to hate, and although he did not know what or why he hated, it was this hate that led to dark and deep, far-reaching hunger, which could not be sated. Although, the constant consumption of food did help to quiet this seemingly gentle giant.

Except for Rose, the lovely bartender, he'd been alone in the place since it opened at ten a.m. He preferred it that way. But now, it was lunchtime, and other regulars were showing up for their first drink of the day. The tavern served a small selection of simple sandwiches made daily and delivered by Vic's, a diner down the street. They were kept in the refrigerator behind the bar. If you wanted your sandwich hot, it went into the microwave for a few minutes. They also had chips and cheese flavored fish crackers, but they weren't free. Nothing was free. The *Fire in the Hole* did a booming business at lunch and dinner because people didn't feel comfortable going to a bar just to drink, but when food was offered, Rose had suggested to her boss, it made for a perfect excuse to get that drink. Rose was much smarter than she appeared.

Why all the fuss, is what Martin thought—drink, eat, do what you need to do. Life is short. He had already eaten one of each kind of sandwich available that morning and was working on his sixth bowl of fish crackers and his seventh Seagram's and water. He never drank alcohol without eating. It made him dizzy and it could bring up other yearnings—yearnings to cook or damage things. He discovered that fact years ago.

"Hey, Fats, whadaya doin' here so early, campin' out?"

It was Albert. Albert was thin and small; five feet six inches from top to bottom. He worked and drank hard and looked older than his forty-three years. Albert owned the coin *Laundromat* across the street and the building it was housed in—a rooming house from the second floor to the fifth floor. No cooking allowed. Tenants were mostly drunks—usually longshoreman or crewmen on freighters. Baltimore had plenty of both. Albert lived on the sixth floor, which was the top floor. He kept the rooms fairly clean—fumigated twice a year, washed the sheets and towels in the *Laundromat* weekly, swept the halls daily and cleaned the one bathroom on each floor on Tuesdays and Thursdays with a strong solution of *Pine-Sol*. You always knew if it was Tuesday or Thursday by the smell. Albert came to the tavern each day for lunch. Plus, on nights when the Oriole's were in town, he went to the tavern so he could watch the game with some company, although, he didn't like the crowds at the stadium. Albert wore a sweat-stained brown fedora. It came off only when he slept or showered, both rarities, and the smell it carried reminded Martin of elephants or camels at the zoo. Every day, Albert drank four beers with lunch. And when he came to watch a ball game, he drank two boilermakers each inning, one at the top, one at the bottom, more if there was excitement.

There was something about Stoker that scared Albert. He couldn't put his finger on it, but because Albert was so short, it made him feel courageous when he harassed Martin. "Fer chrisakes, Fats, dat barstool is gonna slip up yer ass," he said, and then laughed a raspy smoker's laugh.

Martin was not good at making friends. He was sullen and quiet. His parents caused him to fear people. They told him he was the Devil's child because he was much smarter than his parents, who ran a small chicken farm in Hagerstown when Martin was a boy. He read and learned things in school that they thought no one should ever learn because Blanch and Hardy Stoker were religious fanatics. They told Martin he'd burn in hell for his intellectual arrogance and after he graduated law school they went all out and finally got to him. His mother said she was going on a hunger strike to protest his academic accomplishments. He begged her to eat, but she wouldn't. He gave up his job at a prestigious Washington law firm, where he'd made a reputation in an unwanted court- assigned case by successfully defending several leftists accused by the FBI in a complex arson scandal. He moved back home, trying to convince his mother to eat, but she said he couldn't take back all of his education and within a few months she died from starvation, he thought. Afterward, his father accused him of murdering his mother. Hardy would say it first thing in the morning when Martin helped him feed the chickens, and he'd say it last thing at night when he stoked up the wood stove to keep the old farm-house warm as they slept. On one of those nights, Martin couldn't sleep and he found his mother's death certificate and discovered in the space marked, *cause of death*, the words 'ovarian' and 'cancer'. So, Martin moved out, again, and took the first available job he could find. It was at the Federal Bureau of Weights and Measures. That's when things started to go bad for him, when the weight began to accumulate on his bones and the desire to scorch things on large open fires took hold of him. He was also drinking heavily at the time.

Martin Stoker thought Albert was a cruel, shallow, and ignorant little man. Albert always called him 'Fats," and reminded Martin of his father. Martin had been coming to this gin mill for a year because the one he used to go to when he needed to drink—the one he visited for almost twenty-two years—burned down. It happened during a time when Martin was trying to lose weight. Dieting was very difficult because it magnified the hatred, as did the fact that Martin believed he'd never have a relation-ship with a woman because first it was his parents, and then it was the fat. The owner of that other bar, the one that burned, had a drinking prob-lem. When he got drunk, he'd call Martin a fat fag. He died in the fire. They had to identify him from dental records.

Martin edited statutes at Weights and Measures. The hours and the pay were good, but it wasn't challenging because Martin Stoker had gradu-ated, *summa cum laude*, from Virginia Tech in 1953 and, *magna cum laude*, from Georgetown Law School in '56. He wasn't fat back then. He was tall and handsome and athletic. Martin first moved out of the farmhouse in 1949 when he got a football scholarship to college. He thought it might rescue him from his parents—from the fasting and the beatings to cleanse his soul. Martin was bigger than his father by the time he was fifteen, but he thought he needed or deserved the beatings until he read Dickens and Melville in the high school library. After that, Martin became a great football player because the fasting and the beatings had made him tough, and besides, he discovered that he loved to knock peo-ple down. In his senior year at Virginia Tech, he was an All-American linebacker. Martin's back was still covered with scars from the whip his father had used on him.

"You're a mean man, Albert. What do you know about being fat? You better be careful because you don't have any idea what you're messing with," Martin said.

"I'm shakin' in my boots, Fats."

"Look, Albert, just let him drink in peace, will you," Rose said, and she walked over to Martin. She stopped chewing and snapping her gum for a moment and leaned across the bar so she could whisper to him. "Ya wanna sit at a table, Mr. Stoker?"

"Thanks anyway, Rose. I'll be leaving in a few minutes—as soon as I finish this drink." Martin liked saloons with female bartenders. It was like a date, without having to ask.

Rose liked Martin Stoker. He came in once a week, usually on a Friday, drank quietly, was polite, always left a generous tip on the bar, and ran up a bill of thirty or forty bucks. Albert, on the other hand, was a beer drinker. He nursed his two or three beers and left a quarter or maybe, on a rare day, two quarters. She turned and frowned at Albert. "Why don't you behave yourself, little fella?" Then she winked all sexy at him just to keep him confused.

Albert liked Rose. She was thirty-something and she had a fine body. She wore blue jeans, spiked heals, and tight fitting low-cut jerseys when she worked. The jeans showed off her perfect ass, and the jerseys her perfect cleavage, and even her nipples when the air-conditioning got too far ahead of the temperature. (Martin had a good look when she leaned over to whisper to him.) Albert had fantasies about Rose; bedtime fantasies that played a major role in the only sex-life Albert knew. So it hurt his feelings when Rose called him a little man because he believed this was the reason he never could get into a woman's pants, including Rose's.

"Sure. Dat's right. You stand up fer Fats, why dontcha. But tell 'im he's gonna die young if he don't lose weight, Rosy, or areya scared he won't leaveya da usual big tip?" Albert said.

7

"Albert, you're no gentleman," Martin said. "You attack everyone. It's called a Napoleon complex."

"Fuck you and Napoleon," Albert said.

Martin rose from the barstool. "Look you ignorant savage, don't speak like that in front of a lady," he said.

"Rosy here? She ain't no lady, Fats. Showsya how much you know."

"Apologize, Albert," Martin said, and he made a fist with his right hand that was almost the size of Albert's head.

"Like I says, *fuck you*, Fats."

For his fifty years and four hundred and forty-two pounds, Martin moved quickly. He got Albert in a headlock—both his feet dangling above the floor—in seconds. The brim of Albert's fedora was folded down over his ears by Martin's gigantic arm. He looked like Popeye in a baby bonnet. Albert tried to kick Martin.

"Kick me and I'll snap your neck like a toothpick," Martin said. "Now apologize."

Rose came out from behind the bar. She had a baseball bat in her left hand. "Boys," she said, and she placed her right hand on her hip, "Enough!" Then she looked Martin straight in the eye and said, "Put him down before you kill him."

Martin slowly lowered Albert to the floor and released him.

"Ya fat prick, I oughtta sue yer fat ass," Albert yelled as he removed the fedora and reshaped it.

"Albert! Shut up," Rose said.

Albert looked at her and then kicked over a barstool and stormed out.

"I'm sorry," Martin said to Rose.

Rose walked back behind the bar and leaned the bat against the side of the refrigerator. "You surprised me," she said.

"I hate men who are disrespectful to ladies."

"Well, thanks for the taste of chivalry, Mr. Stoker, but I hear language all the time in this joint. It's part of the job." Then she smiled a broad toothy smile, like in toothpaste ads, and said, "But I do appreciate the thought."

"You know, I wasn't always a big fat slob," he said.

She walked around to the front of the bar and picked up the stool Albert had kicked over. Martin couldn't help a quick sideways glance at her perfect heart-shaped ass. Rose's long straight blond hair fell forward as she bent to lift the stool and Martin began imagining things he didn't want to imagine. Then she walked behind the bar, picked up a cloth and wiped some glasses. Martin knew she didn't want to hear his story; no one did, so he pulled a hundred dollar bill from his pocket and placed it on the bar. She totaled his bill: one BLT, one sausage and pepper sandwich, one ham and cheese on white, one fried egg sandwich, four bowls of fish crackers and seven Seagram's and water. "That's twenty-nine and a quarter," she said.

"I had six bowls of crackers, not four," Martin said.

"That's okay. They're on me." She smiled and handed him his change. He left a ten on the bar. She was already serving another customer and apologizing about the fight as he walked out the door.

Albert didn't like being pushed around. He didn't like being picked up like a sack of potatoes. When he was younger—always being a little guy—he learned to use a knife to protect himself in the tough neighborhood where he grew up. He still had his old switchblade and when he left the tavern, he went to his apartment to get it. He was waiting for Martin outside the gin mill door.

"How...daya like... dis, ya big fat... shit," he said, still breathing hard from the run up and down six flights. Then, he stuck Martin in the abdomen with that knife.

Martin felt the burning sting of the blade. He grabbed Albert's wrist and broke it. The knife fell to the ground and Albert cried out in pain. Rose heard Albert shouting and ran out of the bar to see Martin holding his abdomen—the bloodstain growing on his yellow shirt. She saw the bloody knife resting on the sidewalk and Albert on his knees, holding a limp right wrist with his left hand.

The blade of that knife was four inches long and Martin's fat was almost four inches thick so only the tip cut into his abdominal cavity, but it nicked an artery and Martin almost bled to death. Rose thought fast, used some clean bar-cloths and her belt hooked to Martin's to tie around his belly and apply pressure. The doctor's said she saved Martin's life. Martin went to Johns Hopkins University Hospital where the surgeon on call that afternoon was also doing some new experimental surgery for morbid obesity.

"As long as I'm in there," he said, "why don't you let me staple your stomach so it can't hold so much food. You'll lose lots of weight and feel much better."

Albert went to jail for assault with a deadly weapon. Rose told Martin that Albert was going to lose his building and *Laundromat* because he had no one to run it while he was in jail.

She told him this while he was recovering from the surgery because Rose visited Martin at the hospital every day.

"I'll run it for him," he said. "I did provoke him." Martin had two years of unused sick days coming to him. Government jobs are good that way. So he took a leave of absence and moved into Albert's sixth floor apartment. Every day for the next eighteen months he negotiated those stairs many times. As promised, the surgery worked and his fat shrank. He lost almost two hundred pounds. He still needed to eat, but he couldn't get more than a few mouthfuls down at a time because his stomach was all stapled up and only held a small amount of food, so, Martin got full very quickly. He ate ten or twelve times a day and sometimes he chewed and spit it out, but the total quantity swallowed amounted to less than one full meal.

The whole situation, in a way, turned into a kind of godsend. Rose loved the way Martin looked at two-forty and he had loads of money, it seemed to her, which he did because he'd never married, had no extravagances except the food, and of course his father had died in a fire that consumed the farmhouse, so, Martin got the insurance and the proceeds from the sale of sixty prime acres in Hagerstown, near the Interstate. But Martin was a little uneasy. Although eating all the food he could eat and still

10

losing weight, he was beginning to feel unsettled. He was actually losing his appetite. He'd even been going to a gym to workout, to dissipate the uneasiness—the need to cook or damage things.

"Really! You're losing your appetite?" Rose said, as Martin sat at the bar telling her how he felt. She was feeling his biceps. "Wow. you're really getting fit. How old did you say you were?"

"Fifty-one—almost fifty-two, and yes, I'm losing my interest in food, but I have this desire to cook things, especially flesh—meat. I never feel this way when I'm hungry and eating. This need to cook only hits me at certain times," he said.

"Go to a culinary arts school. Become a chef!" Rose said, and she was leaning way over the bar and Martin was getting aroused.

Rose definitely had this idea that Martin was loaded with money and she kind of liked him. So, actually, looking at the various possibilities for her future, she was getting lots of ideas. "Why not come over to my place tonight and show me how you cook. I've got a great grill and you can do something fancy on a nice big fire. Just give me the money and tell me what to buy, and I'll get it on the way home. I'm done here at four."

Albert was paroled for good behavior after eighteen months of his three-year term (his lawyer plea-bargained). He returned home, Martin moved out, and the entire building burned down, *Laundromat* and all. It was an old building, and Albert, apparently, had been paying off the city inspectors, so the wiring was not up to code. That was the cause of the five-alarm blaze, according to the fire inspector, who said that Albert's body looked like a slice of charred bacon.

Next, the doctor called Martin and said the staples had to come out. "More than two years is dangerous," he said.

This statement made Martin, who seemed to be mourning Albert, uncomfortable. "Define dangerous," Martin said, and he laughed. He was sure that if the staples went, his fat would be back or other stuff might come up.

"Don't worry about it, Sweetie," Rose told him. "You've got me now."

The staples came out and he really tried not to eat. He worked out diligently at the gym and also below, behind, beside and above Rose—they were inseparable. Martin liked Rose to stay at home, so she did. They had a few drinks at home because Rose made it nice to drink at home. Martin went to culinary arts school where he developed extraordinary techniques for cooking meats over open flames. In 1980 they were married and they opened a restaurant. Martin called it *Cooking with Fire* as a kind reminder of his love for Rose and of his flaws. It was very successful and for some reason, no one ever wondered about those other fires. Every night Rose kissed the scars on Martin's back and life just went on—that was that.

CLOUDS' ILLUSIONS

Sophia, my third wife, wanted to redecorate the family room, so we went to a fabric and notions shop looking for ideas. The salesman, an older fellow with thick glasses, was standing before shelves crowded with bolts of exotic cloth. He starts right off talking about colors and light. He says light changes the way colors will or will not blend and that this determines what is or is not pleasing to the eye. He looked and sounded very authoritative with his head of wild white hair.

Being a college physics teacher, the manner in which we see fascinates me, so his comments trigger thoughts about particles and waves, which, in my mind, always lead to duality and relativity and the connection between time and light. I'm sixty-something and trying to avoid retirement. Bizarre, far-reaching thoughts show up in my head like driftwood on an incoming tide. Right there in the fabric store an axiom pops into my mind—*what is seen is what the observer is looking for*—and at that exact moment, I remember Ezra Romano....

Many years ago, we were best friends and this sudden recall takes me back to a short interval when we were young enough to play pretend, but old enough to notice girls. I remember how we'd imagine ourselves rescuing beautiful young maidens in distress, grabbing them up and carrying them off to safety on great white chargers. We were too young to know for sure, but we sensed by some, as yet dormant instinct, the possibility of reward. Sometimes, mostly in dreams, I still sense that feeling and thinking about it reminds me that, back then, I believed Ezra and I would always be best friends and, also, that romantic love would be a cornerstone in my life.

Just before college, a war got started and we believed we'd wind up there because my older brother was called. Having to fight, kill and perhaps, get killed, nagged at us. So, we decided to have fun in college where sex, love, and alcohol all blended together into a process. For example, once Ezra hired two beautiful female escorts and we took them to a fraternity costume ball. They dressed like damsels—long whooped skirts, veils, and tall pointed hats. We dressed like jesters because we couldn't find knight's attire, anywhere. At first I was embarrassed and even felt a little guilty because Ezra and I had girlfriends, but then I smiled about that night, remembering how after the ball, pretend became reality and uncovered-rewards.

Of course, we never told our girlfriends, Joyce and Carmen (who was a sweet and beautiful girl); never told them about that night or the many others shared with young women looking to be rescued. Ezra and I were, for the most part, honest with each other, but, in those days, we were unfaithful to the girls.

Actually, Ezra was worse than most of us—I mean about loyalty, which is why it surprised me that he and Carmen stuck it out as long as they did. When they married during senior year of college, Carmen was pregnant. I know I tried to talk Carmen out of marrying Ezra, but she did it anyway. Ezra was lucky. Besides his father being very rich, he got Carmen, *and* he didn't get drafted after college. I went to that damned war in Southeast Asia, which I don't think did me a lot of good because, although I survived, when I got back I was a different person, disappointed and very angry. After awhile, I married Joyce. I suppose we *were* friends. We often sat, over tea, and talked about almost anything. *Almost*, being the keyword, because things that seemed to really matter, like love and sex and peace of mind, never entered the conversation. I didn't love Joyce.

And life with her was mostly lonely, with or without tea, because I never felt her feeling anything. So, I kept on being unfaithful with girls who did. I was looking for romance, for passion, but Joyce—wife number one—was cold and distant.

The marriage counselor suggested that I married her because she was safe. And Carmen, who was always close with Joyce, said the same thing. She said, "Bobby, life is a crap-shoot. Joyce may be a cold fish, but you'll always know where you stand with a girl like *her*." I think she also said something about the complexity of passionate women in romantic relationships, but I'm not certain. Carmen and I could talk about anything. I can't recall when this conversation with Carmen actually took place, although, I have some vague memory of being very unhappy about my brother—did I mention that my older brother died in Vietnam when I was a senior in college? Carmen was so kind and compassionate about my brother's death. She tried to comfort me and I thought she loved me because she behaved differently with me than she did with Ezra, but I can't hold on to any images or feelings, for some reason. I only remember that she was determined to marry into Ezra's family when she turned up pregnant. So, after graduation, I volunteered for Vietnam and I don't know why I did.

Anyway, Joyce finally divorced me and it was for the best. We didn't have any kids, either, which was probably because we rarely had sex. Sex with Joyce—it's not worth discussing—but having no children was the good thing. Still, she, or something, left holes in me that occasionally leak and make me list like a torpedoed tramp steamer—did I mention that I was shot in Vietnam? It wasn't pretty, but as I've said, I survived. To this day, I can't seem to separate Joyce, or maybe it's the idea of Joyce, from wasted loveless years, or maybe it's the idea of wasted loveless years. I think I might have become cynical....

So, I can't remember what I had for breakfast this morning, but this stuff is pouring from some forgotten corner of my mind while I'm

17

standing in that small fabric store. I notice that Sophia is explor-
ing fabric and going at it with the salesman and although I'm trying to stay with colors, I can't stop toying with light and friendship,
or maybe it has to do with losing things, or never having them and
two questions start banging around in my head: Is leaving something
behind the same as losing it? Is being rejected the same as leaving
something behind? I'm not good at this sort of thing. For me, trying
to understand feelings is similar to looking into a kaleidoscope and I
don't even like being in the same room as one.

"Hey," wife number three says, "are you still in the here and now?"

"Not exactly," I say. "I was thinking about Ezra Romano—an old
friend."

"Do I know him?" she says, but she doesn't stop her search for the
right swatch.

"I don't think so," I say, "I haven't heard from him in years," and I try
to join her in the hunt for patterns and matching colors.

I notice that I like the look and feel of some fabric more than others.

"Maybe I heard you mention him, because something sounds famil-
iar," she says. "You tried to call Ezra just a few months ago, right?"

"How did you know that?"

She keeps flipping through bolts of cloth and laughs, as if at her
own cleverness, "I heard you talking to what sounded like an answering
machine and you used that name, Ezra, which you have to admit, is quite
unusual. Plus, lately, you've been talking in your sleep...what do you
think of this?" she says in the same breath, and holds up some fabric that
I suspect glows in the dark.

Running it between my thumb and index finger, I notice that it's
very soft and smooth to the touch, and an image of Carmen, young and
beautiful, fills my head. "I'm not sure," I say, and I'm not comfortable
to hear that I talk in my sleep because Sophia has never mentioned
this.

But despite my uncertainty, Sophia has made up her mind. She
points to the bolt of red fabric and says, "This one."

18

The spectacled salesman says, "What an excellent shade of red, and in such a richly textured fabric." Then, he adjusts his glasses and adds, parenthetically, "Just remember the light."

Sophia looks at me, "Do you think he's right about light?" she says.

"Maybe," I say, but my mind is still on sleep-talk and, Carmen.

"We need to make a decision, Bobby. I'm hungry. Give me your best guess and let's get on with it."

Sophia has been a wonderful partner. She gets to the heart of any matter. She's decisive, while I'm more inclined to mull and dwell and avoid confrontations or things that aren't pleasant. Sophia swears that I can actually convince myself unpleasant things never happened. "Okay, let's say he's right," I say. "If you like the way the fabric looks here, maybe we need to use the same light bulbs in the family room. At least that's what I think...unless—"

"Good idea," she says and the salesman smiles. I notice that he looks older than me, or perhaps he's had a tougher life.

We buy the new fabric for drapes in the family room, and some special custom light bulbs, which they use and sell at *True Colors*, the fabric store, because it has no windows. Then we leave the store and catch a cab—ask the driver to take us to our favorite restaurant, the *Paper Moon Café*, where they serve 'fusion' cuisine—the sort of food you wouldn't normally imagine because it combines the unanticipated—Cajun-New England curried fish stew with risotto, or Texas-Polynesian pizza topped with fried oysters, garlic butter and pineapple. These are our favorite *Paper Moon* dishes. The sign on the door suggests that experiencing unusual taste combinations releases the mind. At first I found the idea disturbing, but when I tried the fish stew it was liberating.

As we ride across town in the taxi, Sophia rests her head on the seatback, her once lovely brown eyes close and I can't help noticing that she's looking much older. Her cheeks flop from side to side like bloodhound jowls as the cab hits potholes, and her lower lip flutters when she exhales. I'm wondering how I must appear to her when I'm asleep. "I talk in my sleep?" I ask.

"Oh, it's nothing. Just forget it, Bobby."

But I'm not sure I can forget it, until, I remember the great margaritas at the *Paper Moon*, which come in a fishbowl with two straws. Ordinarily, Sophia wouldn't drink alcoholic beverages. She says she doesn't like to lose control and I understand this, because I've never liked losing anything. However, Sophia loves those margaritas. She says it's the fishbowl idea with two straws that really gets to her more than the taste.

I'm looking out the window of the cab, watching shadows lengthen. I'm worried about the sort of things I might say, later on, in my sleep. Then I notice a fly in the taxi. It buzzes about and runs into windows like they aren't there, finally stunning itself, and falling to the floor between my feet. I'm careful to avoid crushing it as it makes a different kind of sound and rolls in circles. This noise and motion depress me. We arrive at the Café and as soon as I open the cab door, that fly takes off. I watch it till it disappears and my mood improves.

Inside the *Paper Moon,* we find a good place to sit, order a fishbowl and hold hands across the table. I notice our age-spots. In the *Paper Moon*, everything is black and white—tables, floors, walls, even the waiters' uniforms, but they have these moving filters over the lights in four shades of purple, so the place and everything in it keeps changing colors. And there's always music. At the moment, it's Judy Collins singing a song that I like about clouds and love and life, *"I've looked at clouds from both sides now...."* Our fishbowl comes and I'm listening to the words of the song and looking at Sophia. I remember how pretty she was when she was young, when her hair was long and auburn—beautiful dark eyes—I didn't know her then. Now she colors her hair because it's mostly gray, and she keeps it short. I'm watching the age spots on our hands disappear as the room passes through shades of mauve, when right out of the blue Sophia stops sucking on the straw and says,

"I'll bet he's not happy."

"Where did that come from?" I say and I'm startled enough to almost lose control of my bladder, which is a recent and annoying problem that leaves telltale evidence in my under-shorts.

"I heard a fly trapped in the cab, on the way over here," she says, "and it made me think about Ezra. No one just drops an old friend without a reason—like they can't come to terms with some part of their *own* life, or maybe they were *never* a friend to begin with...do you really like this fabric?" she adds, pulling a corner out of the bag. But in the light of the *Paper Moon*, the color is nondescript and I'm at a loss for words. "Now what was I talking about?" she says after a few silent moments pass. Sophia is getting a little senile but I don't mention it because it's a touchy subject.

"I can't tell in here," I say, "but it looked good at the fabric store," and then I'm thinking, wow, I never saw it that way....

Maybe Ezra never was my friend or Joyce for that matter, or maybe I don't understand what friendship is about, or even love. Ezra and I often talked about the kind of women we'd like to marry and about our friendship, "Like brothers," we'd always say. *I don't know how much Ezra really loved Carmen. He never said, and when I got back from Vietnam, Ezra and Carmen were in trouble because Ezra was up to his old tricks.* Carmen divorced him. She went to live overseas—someplace far off and unreachable—and she took the boy, who, it turned out, was not Ezra's son, which apparently really pissed Ezra off, particularly when he did the numbers. I guess I knew that, too, but I really couldn't see how it mattered because Ezra and the boy believed they were father and son until Carmen let the cat out of the bag. *I didn't think she needed to bring that up and God knows what else she told him.* Carmen was such a beautiful, passionate young woman. I was still married to Joyce when they divorced.

Anyway, I never got to see much of the boy—he called me Uncle Bobby. A short while later, Joyce divorced me because she said she knew I didn't love her. Life was not working out the way I thought it would. So many empty years, like willows in winter. My parents passed during that time—smoked themselves to death—and everything was jumbled up in my head. I finally went back to school and got a masters degree in physics. I chose physics, instead of history or psychology, because it better suits my personality.

When I was forty-something, I ran into Ezra, again. We both had new wives and as I recall, it seemed to be the greatest thing—I mean to find an old friend after so much loneliness. Seeing him was like remembering you can swim in the middle of a dream where you're going down for the last time. I was married to wife number two and we had a couple of kids, but it wasn't going well. I still felt close to Ezra, remembering how we once cared about and planned our lives—how it gave us a sense of orientation. He didn't seem to be as happy about running into me.

And I wasn't careful about what I said—I didn't think I needed to be. Maybe that was the problem because when he commented on how much my new wife looked like Carmen, I said something about his new wife being very lovely, too, which she truly was. I wanted to reminisce with Ezra, but it was like the past did not exist for him. I'll be damned if I know exactly what it was that I did or said, but after only a year or so, Ezra was gone, *again*.

I wrote him a letter and told him how much our friendship meant to me. I said that maybe I had behaved badly and apologized for whatever I might have done, past or present. He never answered the letter....

Sitting there in the *Paper Moon*, I'm feeling nervous—unsettled. Why am I remembering this stuff? My mind won't stop trying to put it together—first it's wife number one, then it's Ezra, and then it's wife number two (which I'll get to)—maybe it *is* me.

Maybe, I'm some kind of *serious* asshole. Right then, as if she's reading my mind, Sophia says, "It's really simple. If a person is an asshole, who wants to be around them?" She says, "Bobby, you're no asshole. Sometimes you're a pain in the ass, but there is a difference. No, My Love," she says, "that Ezra is under some very bad karma,"—and she gets that smirk again, "I'll bet you remind him of something he needs to forget," and she laughs.

I'm focused on the asshole thing. "You're pretty sure I'm not an asshole?" I say.

"Yep," she says, and then sucks up a big mouthful of margarita.

22

I really want to find relief in Sophia's observation, but I sense an edge on things. I order another fishbowl, and the curried fish stew. Sophia orders the pizza with extra Parmesan cheese, but she asks the waiter to hold the garlic butter because it gives her cramps and I wish she hadn't mentioned the cramps to him. We're sitting there, working on the second fishbowl, lost in our own thoughts. We smile at each other and I notice that although her eyes are still quite beautiful, she has hair growing on her upper lip and wrinkles on her skin that make her face and neck look like Death Valley. I'm wondering when we both got so old. I go to the men's room to empty my bladder. I see my face in the mirror. I'm almost wrinkle-free. When I return, I find myself still looking at Sophia's face.

"What?" she says.

I'm afraid she's reading my mind, again. "You're just so pretty," I say, but it's Carmen I'm remembering—maybe it's the margaritas. Then it hits me! If I *were* an asshole, how could Sophia love me? That's *exactly* right, because she's not your average everyday female. No, Sophia is intact—she'd been around. She was smart, and used to be a real beauty, herself—"Miss Congeniality," in the 1958 Miss Kansas beauty pageant.

She still has the trophy in a box up in the attic (I know this because I go look at it sometimes and the pictures of her in her bathing suit and evening gown, which bear no resemblance to her present-day appearance). Years later, she ran a huge toxic waste management business her first husband left to her. She ran it for almost a decade and then sold it for a very big profit. Sophia is rich. *And,* what's really important is that Sophia came after *me.* That's right! I remember it, perfectly: Back then I'm a bachelor, divorced from wife number two, who ran off with this Mafia stud. No joke. They show up together one day at the house, him in a shiny green suit and her all over him, and she says, "This is Vincent Gorgonzola, (or something that sounded like that at the time), and I'm running away with him."

I just let them go because guys with names like that can get rough and besides, wife number two was a drunk. She tells me that if I will take the kids, she'll just leave—no alimony, no nothing. Naturally, I keep the kids and it turns out to be a good thing for all of us. We never hear from her again.

Six or seven months after wife number two departed with Vinnie, some neighbors invite me to a party. I guess they're feeling sorry for me. At the time, I'm a late forty-something and teaching physics at State College, where younger women continue to give me looks. These neighbors also invited a friend of theirs, Sophia Bates, to this party because Sophia's husband had died from cancer some years before and I guess they're trying to play matchmaker. She's rich and smart and quite attractive for an older broad but no matter, because at the time I'm definitely not looking for another relationship. I've already lost too much, including wife number two—her name was Ginger—but I still had the kids, which was a good thing. Sophia, however, had other ideas and I'm not sure if it was me—you know, being desirable, or vulnerable or pathetic...or maybe it was the kids—a boy and a girl, five and seven, and very sweet—Sophia never had kids.

At the time, Sophia's friends are telling her she's nuts wanting to start over with me, wanting to raise my kids. I'm a two-time loser. But Sophia tells them that *I* will make the difference. That's exactly what she told me, "*Bobby*, you will make the difference." And this moved me because Sophia acted like I was somebody, like I really meant something to her. Plus, she tells me not to miss out on her. She said, "Don't miss out on me, Bobby," just like that. Then she bought me a black *Turbo Carra* for an engagement present, which I still drive. It's a classic, now.

I have to admit, back then, it was not a woman like Sophia that I dreamed about. She was quite a few years older than me and I was worried and unsure of myself. But, she was a wonderful person and I thought maybe it could all work out. What did I have to lose?

Although—and this is difficult for me to admit—sometimes I still think of Carmen and then this helpless, lonely feeling comes over me and I don't understand. But it's not important. What is important is this: Last September, at our nineteenth-anniversary party, some of Sophia's friends said, "Bobby will make the difference, he'll make life so grand," and they laughed and pointed at me, as if it weren't true. But I guess Sophia saw something in me that I didn't and they still don't. I'm glad because we've been together almost twenty years. It's been a different experience for me and the two kids, who are all grown up now and living lives of their own, they call her 'Mother,' and they mean it....

So, sitting there in the Paper Moon, I say, "Sophia, I do make the difference, right?" and I laugh because I realize that it's an odd question.

She's eating her pizza and there's some cheese stuck in the corner of her mouth. "What?" she says.

"Remember when we first got together, your friends thought you were nuts for wanting to marry me and raise my kids, and you said that I'd make it worthwhile?"

We decide to order a third fishbowl and the waiter looks at us kind of funny because he's too young to understand.

"Is it true?" I ask her.

"Is what true?"

"That I make the difference, for christsake."

"Where the heck did that come from?" Sophia says, and now, she's giggling.

Like I've said, Sophia isn't accustomed to booze, she's usually all orderly and tight, like a well made bed, but the margaritas are having their effect. I remind her of the story and she says, "Oh. Sure, I remember." But she keeps eating and then she grabs at her stomach and says, "Shit."

"What?" I say, and I'm worried because Sophia is a healthy woman, and she almost never says 'shit.'

"I think they put garlic butter on my burger."

"That's pizza," I say, and then I see a couple of tears sneaking down her cheek. "Honey, what's the matter, is it the garlic butter?" I say, and I reach for her hand but she pulls it away.

"Not really," she says. "It's that sometimes you're so sweet, telling me I'm pretty when I'm really an old senile lizard, and besides, I know who you really...." She stops in mid-sentence and starts to cry.

25

I'm sure the margaritas are getting to her. "I just want you to be happy," I say, and then for some reason add, "but I keep wondering about this thing with—Ezra."

Sophia stops crying as fast as she started and looks at me for what seems like a long time. The place goes through several color changes and the music stops. It is in this quiet that Sophia speaks with a very loud voice, "Look Bobby, just *fuck* Ezra. It's over and done."

She startles me. And naturally, some of the other customers hear her, and they're looking our way. "I'm sorry," I say. I smile at them. The manager comes over to our table. "Excuse me, *folks*, but is everything in order here?" His face is a kind of violet color and he seems to be intentionally ignoring Sophia.

"*Fuck you, too, sonny,*" Sophia says to him.

"Now honey—" I start to say.

"Don't 'now honey' me, you *asshole*," she says. Then she gets this terrible look on her face and runs for the lady's room with a hand over her mouth. The music starts up again, and it's Tony Bennett singing, "*It's only a paper moon, hanging in a cardboard sky....*"

That was the last time we went to the *Paper Moon Café*. I guess Sophia was humiliated and although it's been months, I still don't know what got into her. I thought, at first, it was garlic butter and margaritas, but she said that was only part of the problem, and she hasn't said anymore. I'm back to my doubts—you know, with the 'asshole' thing. Every time we sit in the family room with those new light bulbs and the red drapes, I'm just not sure of anything. What has my life been about? Was it me or Ezra—me, or those other wives? Why do I always feel like something is missing? I have more questions than answers. *And*, I'm still worried about talking in my sleep, although, I can't raise that subject with Sophia because it makes me too uncomfortable.

One Sunday morning, however, we're in the family room and I'm kind of losing it. I say, "Sophia, life is so damned complicated"—the words just jump out of my mouth.

Sophia's doing the crossword puzzle in the *Times* and she doesn't even look up. She just says, "It's not, Bobby. You forget that time marches on, My Love. The past is past. We've all made our mistakes... what's a five letter word for forbidden?"

"Apple," I say. But I can't seem to let it go because I don't know what needs letting go. I wish we had never gone to that fabric store, or at least never heard what that salesman had to say about light determining what is or is not pleasing. I keep remembering the axiom—*what is seen is what the observer is looking for*—and lately I've been wondering if that's connected with, '*what you don't accept, you don't allow to happen,*' which I read someplace else. But the worst thing is I can't seem to get to it—whatever *it* is. I believe it has something to do with Ezra, or maybe, with being an asshole. I'm thinking it has to do with something I can't control, when Sophia interrupts my thoughts:

"Bobby," she says, "I'm getting tired of looking at our bedroom. It's time to redecorate."

Her words have an odd effect on me (the bladder thing). "The fabric store again?" I say.

"Tomorrow," she says, "and you don't have any classes because it's Washington's Birthday. They're even having a sale."

"Do I really talk in my sleep?"

"Oh, Bobby, grow up. You don't have to keep saying it's about Ezra when it's about Carmen," she says. "I know that."

"Carmen!" I say, and I'm stunned. "How could it be about Carmen?"

"Well, silly me," she says. "What do I know? I'm just a senile old coot."

Then Sophia's back in her newspaper, and I'm headed for the bathroom and a change of underwear. I'm thinking I'll be damned if I'll ever wear those diapers for old people. Who knew getting old would be like this. I try to remind myself that the past is the past and I can't do a thing about it. But I don't even know where Carmen is *or what's become of the boy and I wonder how she looks, now, because I only remember her as beautiful.* I hope there's a pill for this damned bladder thing. *How old would he be now, forty-something?* I walk out of the family room and turn into the dimness of the hallway that leads to the master bedroom and bath. It is in this low light that another question begins to bang around in my head: Is there a difference between me, and my idea of me?

THE ALIBI

.....There isn't one of you in this room would recognize love if it
stepped up and buggered you in the ass...

Raymond Carver

According to my shrink I've been hiding all these years because the love
in my life never added up to what I hoped for. I say disappointment. She
says anger and resentment. For years I've heard her repeat, "At some
point, Jimmy, you'll need to get over it," which is one reason I made
the last minute decision to attend my forty-year college reunion back in
Indiana. The other was CJ, the wife of my college roommate, Tom. She
died unexpectedly a month before the reunion. My shrink thought the
trip was a mistake. "Make up your mind," I said and my shrink said, "No,
you make up yours."

Me? I've been living in the Pacific Northwest since the 70s, running a hostel for hikers in the mountains east of Seattle. I find people
who like to walk mountain-trails easy to deal with. And whenever there's
some extra money, four or five times a year maybe, I visit the shrink and
although I'm not crazy about Doctor Jane Armour, she's only an hour

ride from the hostile and charges what I can afford. Besides, it's the talking that helps. Hell, sometimes I just talk out loud to myself.

The day Tom called from Indiana to tell me CJ had died of a heart attack his voice was wobbly and hearing that news, so was mine. I knew I needed to visit him, and figured I could kill two birds with one stone since I received the notice for the reunion around the same time. Tom didn't intend to go to the reunion. "Too much pain," he said but he offered me a place to sleep. We hadn't seen one another since graduation but kept in touch with the usual notes scribbled on the back of Christmas cards, even when I was overseas, speaking of which, Tom was lucky back then—avoided Vietnam because when he married CJ there was an instant deferment. CJ was special. She was a dream-girl.

So, I bought the ticket to Indiana, was even excited about the trip, but as it turned out, after several days of visiting it was good I had to leave for the reunion because Tom wasn't bathing or changing his clothes and the house was filthy. He was a slob back in college and now depression set in and he was worse. Losing CJ was terrible for him but I was finished thinking about it. I wanted to remember her in a certain way, maybe remember everything in a certain way—that dream-girl image tucked away in my head; the one I formulated the first time I saw Kim Novak dance with William Holden in *Picnic*. I own that movie on videotape. I first saw *Picnic* in '55, but I could never get that scene out of my head—the way Novak looked and moved; the way they fell hopelessly in love. Novak was a dream-girl. I was fourteen. I wrote her a love letter—addressed it to Kim Novak, Hollywood, California. I never got an answer.

As I drove to the reunion my mind was searching for college-memories of CJ. The top was down and wind was clearing my head when I went for the special hand-lever designed for handicapped drivers like me who can't use their feet to operate brake or accelerator pedals. Tires squealed, road-grit flew, and the guy behind me blew his horn and almost rear-ended the gimp-equipped Malibu I was able to rent at Indianapolis airport. I drove onto the shoulder and he flipped me a bird but I didn't care because I was focusing on a structure I hadn't seen in years—the converted barn roadhouse where we gathered to drink and dance during junior and senior year in college. Now, it was all boarded up, the parking lot overgrown with weeds, even the sign on the roof was in ruins, bright red paint, faded, and missing two large neon letters. AL_B_ it said in a kind of washed-out burgundy on flaking sooty gray, but back then that *Alibi* sign turned the night sky red on an otherwise dark stretch of Route 37 north of Bloomington, Indiana. I moved the car from the shoulder into ragweed and knee-high grass.

Regan Browne was on my mind. I met her at the *Alibi*. A few boards were missing among the ones nailed across the front entrance and it looked like enough space for me to slip through. I put the top up, shut off the engine and got out of the car. I could see the *Alibi's* front doors were open behind the boards and I climbed through using my arms to guide the heavy prostheses that hung from the stumps where my legs used to be. Inside, I waited a moment for my eyes to adjust to the dimness, then walked down the five plank steps and stood dead still at the bottom.

The only light slid in through thin spaces created by warping boards that had been nailed over the windows years before—fine laser-like beams that shot to the booths, the bar, and the bandstand. The place was still, except for dust particles that danced in the light-beams. Things were broken—a table here, a window there, the mirrors behind the bar. The floor was covered with pieces of torn newspaper that looked like confetti. It was eerie but I knew how to defend myself. Losing my legs in Vietnam didn't mean I forgot the basic skills of hand-to-hand combat they taught me in Special Warfare School. I always carry a pocketknife with a four-inch blade.

I brushed away cobwebs and dust from a chair with the wool scarf I wear around my neck when the weather turns cold. Coats are too cumbersome. I sat at the end of a nearby booth and the sound of my stainless steel knees folding into flexion echoed in the empty *Alibi*. I was thinking about change; what had and what hadn't. The last time I was in the *Alibi* there was music playing and skin ran all the way down my legs into my shoes. There were different ideas in my head. I opened the pocketknife and stuck it into the tabletop....

"Hey Regan, want to go to the *Alibi* this weekend?" I'd say.

"Who's asking," she'd say. "Do you know how lucky you'd be if I said yes?" she'd say.

Regan Browne happened on the rebound from a painful break-up with Patty, my high school sweetheart, my dream girl. Patty went to a different college after we graduated from Crown Point High. We kept in touch for several years and saw one another at holidays and summer breaks until I heard she was fucking for an upper classman at Northwestern. I was stunned and for months cried myself to sleep over the loss. But weeks of implacable sorrow slipped into jealousy and finally, rage. In a well-meaning act of mercy, Tom took me to the *Alibi* to relieve my agitated and dangerous state of mind.

"Get on with your life," he said, "There are plenty of other dream girls in the world."

Indiana University was only a thirty-minute drive from the *Alibi* but I had never been to the place when there was a future with Patty. Classes, baseball, and my dream-girl satisfied my needs. In those days I didn't even drink. I was on an athletic scholarship and after graduation hoped to play baseball for the White Sox. I was a great infielder and a long ball hitter with a future in professional baseball. On one of those early *Alibi* visits I saw Regan Browne dancing with Tom's girlfriend, CJ. From the way they moved anyone could see those two loved to dance. I boogalooed right out on that dance-floor and joined them, showing off some great moves because dancing was another one of my skills.

And in those early days with Regan I felt lucky because she acted like she was hot shit, with expensive clothing, a fine body, and smart. She wasn't as pretty or as sexy as Patty—didn't press her body against me when we slow-danced the way Patty did. Still, for a while, I enjoyed Regan. But in senior year when graduation was only months away I began to have second thoughts about everything because right after my breakup with Patty, in a foolish fit of passionate patriotism I had volunteered for ROTC and in the spring of senior year the Army said I was going to infantry school as soon as I graduated. There was trouble brewing in Southeast Asia and the Middle East, and there was trouble between me and Regan.

Maybe it was the old *Alibi*, the only sound, car tires rhythmically slapping concrete out on Route 37, or maybe the Brownian movement of dust particles, that chaotic motion caused by atoms slamming into one another, because something was messing with my head, filling it with images from the past...the night Regan brought up marriage: "Do you think we could ever be a married couple, James?" She'd had a few whiskey sours and leaned over the table with a faraway look in her dark brown eyes. Her delicate fingers were patting my left hand as it rested on the table. I had a soda in my right hand and wasn't expecting the question but I remember distinctly she said 'could be'—'do you think we could be.'

"I'd like to grow old with someone and love that person forever," I said and Regan smiled, but I was thinking of Patty because I needed a certain kind of girl at my side. Regan was not a dream-girl and it isn't something explainable. Sure, Regan was sexy when she danced but Patty was sexy all the time—the perfume, long red hair, green eyes, her perfect Kim Novak body and shy seductive smile.

I grew up with *The Donna Reed Show*, *Father Knows Best*, and *The Lone Ranger*. You got the idea that life was sweet and simple. Nothing was too hard to fix if you believed and had some guts. Regan was like Donna Reed. CJ and Patty were like Novak. Still, there was something about her that attracted me, but after going out for a year or so, she said, "James, you have an inside place where I'm not invited." I smiled but in my head a voice said, "And you never will be." The problem had several faces. I preferred girls who weren't so lofty. Or maybe it had to do with the women in her family who made the men in that family wish they were dead.

There was no exception to the misery of the men in Regan's family. They were all drunks. On one occasion of his frequent inebriation her father walked up beside me during a party at the Browne home, took a firm hold of my arm, raised his eyebrows at the mass of my biceps and then whispered, "See all the lovely ladies adorning the room, smelling so sweet? Well, hear me Mr. Jock," he said, "They come with a price." He took a deep drag on his cigarette, coughed hard and stumbled off towards the bar for a refill. He was laughing. "Dry as a bone," he muttered over his shoulder.

No, Regan wasn't at all like Novak and back then, for me, dream girls were more important than a fine car or boat, even a very special infielder's glove with that smell of soft quality leather. I could never be the man I imagined without a dream-girl at my side.

My mother liked Regan, not Patty. She said Patty's family was too "Blue Collar." Mother was an intellectual who was not happily married. She never admitted it, but when she spoke of some writer she had known before marrying my father her eyes said what her mouth apparently couldn't. My dad was a good guy. He repaired tractor engines for a living and his hands were rough and stained with grease—even in his coffin. Still, I usually followed my mother's advice because time so often proved her right. She warned me not to go to war.

And Regan's exclusively Roman-Catholic-girl's-school-education made things worse. A few months after I met her, she told me about nuns saying that slow-dancing was dangerous because boys were likely to get excited and the "devil's shillelagh" would poke at a girl's thighs and lead her into "filthy" temptation, or worse, she could possibly become "pregnant through clothing." Even though Regan laughed at that story, she didn't like slow dancing. Regan was a victim of nuns and the non-secreting females in her family because when it came to sex, Regan showed no interest.

I was raised without religion. Secular hope guided my perspective. Life meant endless possibilities and this may explain why, in spite of all the warning signs, certain feelings on my part developed for Regan. I hoped that by some magic Regan would become a dream-girl and it took longer than expected for me to give up that hope because to be honest, there was something about Regan: how she danced the Boogaloo, the Twist, and the Mashed Potato. She had moves. And there was an expression on her face, like the cat had her tongue.

Her hips, legs, arms, all inviting, breasts jiggling ever so slightly (and in utter innocence) under her sweater. Plus, Mother kept praising Regan. "Such a fine young woman," she said. But Regan was no Patty.

The beams of light moved toward horizontal as the sun worked its way west and then entered from the other side of the *Alibi*. Dust-particle movement slowed and the place took on a kind of sepia tone. I brushed dust off the table and raised a small cloud in which Regan appeared sipping her whiskey sour, then she stared at my right ear with mournful eyes, twirling strands of bleached hair around her right thumb and index finger. She always twirled her hair when she was thinking. She spoke without looking into my eyes, "What are we going to do with our lives, James?" The question sounded sad.

As dust-particles settled back to the table top, I remembered that when she asked, my eyes were on CJ and Tom necking in an adjacent booth and Regan's question interrupted my fantasizing about another occasion at a drive-in movie when I got a glimpse of CJ sucking Tom's dick. Regan and I were laying on the front seat, actually watching the movie, *Bus Stop* with Hope Lange and Marilyn Monroe and CJ's activity was visible through the space between the seatbacks. She saw me looking and her eyes smiled like I could be next as she slid her lovely full lips up and down Tom's stiff dick while Monroe sang "Black Magic."

I reluctantly let go of that CJ-memory and looked at Regan. "We're gonna dance till the music stops," I said, "and I'm going to play short-stop for the White Sox." But I was thinking CJ was a dream girl and Tom was lucky. I was missing Patty.

"No, be serious," Regan said.

"Okay, we could have sex," I said with unusual courage. Unusual because when it came to sex, I was shy until things got going, which was another of Patty's virtues because she moved me beyond the shyness.

"You shut up," Regan said and sort of smiled.

We never discussed having sex and we'd been dating for over a year. I kissed her and after awhile even touched her here and there, but never skin on skin. I couldn't tell if she liked it because she'd get dead still. But her 'shut up' was not a no, which is why I tried with her, just once: Her parents were away on a cruise and that weekend she decided to stay at home instead of the dorm, which I thought was a message. Regan was in her pajamas and we were kissing in her bedroom and I went for skin. It seemed like the right time and place.

"What the hell are you doing?" she said. "You think I'm some kind of goddamned whore?" she said. "You keep your filthy fucking hands to yourself." She ran to the bathroom and cried. Washed her hands for at least ten minutes because she had accidentally touched my dick, which I let out in that moment of desperate need. I felt like such a shit and as I zipped my fly and listened to her crying in the bathroom a powerful emotion formed inside of me. I made a decision to end it with Regan. But a few nights later when we met at the *Alibi* she acted like nothing had happened and I didn't say what I had planned to say. I just said "Hey Regan, wanna dance?" And she said "Is dancing all you can think about?"

"Well no. I *think* about other things," I said, and she said "Get your goddamned mind out of the gutter," and started to walk away but I said "Regan, does it make you sad that I may go to war and die?"

She turned and faced me and I thought I saw tears forming in her eyes. "For Christ's sake, James, I don't want to talk about sorrows," she said, and she put her arms around me and kissed me hard. I decided Regan's steady use of seedy language, unusual for any girl in those days, but particularly a Catholic girl, was a sublimation of sexual need.

Sitting there in the *Alibi* so many years later also brought my Patty to mind. We dated for almost four years—Patty, who loved sex and was so easy to look at; who if she started to flirt with you, sex could happen. Whenever I looked at Patty or even thought about her there was this feeling. It happened the first time we kissed, my heart pounding, everything getting warm and moist. To this day whenever Patty comes to mind something happens. The idea of Patty haunts me because when Patty was kissing me, I needed to touch her—all over. And she'd say, "Mmm," and push her tongue deeper into my mouth—thrust her pelvis against me, "Mmm...Mmmm." It was a soft sound, but firm and certain and full of promise, like the feel of her breasts and erect nipples and she made that sound with her eyes closed and her head slowly nodding 'yes' for more, and 'yes' when the touch was just right and sometimes she'd take my hand and put it where she wanted it, guide my fingers with her fingers. "Mmmmmmmm," she said. "Mmmmmmmmmm," the sound still soft but more intense. And then she cried out as if there was pain and her kiss got harder, her tongue filling my mouth. After, her hand would find my zipper and she knew what to do. *I'd* say, "Oh Baby!" And finally I'd say, "Oh Baby, I love you."

I was too shy to buy condoms even though she wanted me inside of her because we were in love and it was okay if you were in love. But with all the joy, there was a dilemma for me. I guess it was the blue-collar thing, not to mention how you heard a lot about what *nice* girls did and did not do in those days and at certain times I needed Patty to be a nice girl. I did not want anyone, including the pharmacist, to know Patty was having sex with me. At other times I'd almost be in her, or I'd be in and then out. "Oh, Baby, I love you." Although we worried about late periods, the sex obsessed me. I desperately wanted uninhibited sex with Patty in a beautiful bed with privacy and hours to explore her delicious body but it never happened that way.

What did happen was one weekend in sophomore year, Patty and I were both home and she brought a college friend with her who seemed nice but I was disappointed because I had stolen some condoms from Tom's stash, which he kept in a dresser drawer in our dorm room. Patty's friend didn't have much to say until the three of us went to see an old Doris Day movie, also starring James Cagney. It was another '55 movie, but I can't remember the title. I just remember Day singing a song called *I'll Never Stop Loving You.* At intermission Patty went to the ladies room. That was when I heard about her doing it with the upper classman. "Be careful," Patty's friend said, "You're such a sweet guy and she doesn't deserve you. She'll break your heart." Then she touched my face and kissed me—right there in the theater during intermission.

"What are you talking about?" I said when I finally got her tongue out of my mouth and pushed her off.

"She's being unfaithful. He's a senior with his own apartment. You just ask her about Jack Shultz, but don't tell her you heard it from me."

Now this girl was not a looker, not like Patty and I figured maybe she was jealous of us. But then I started thinking it didn't make sense that someone could be so mean as to make something like that up—even the guys name, and why would Patty bring home a friend when we had a chance to be together and have sex? This is how I became jealous and fucked up. Still, Patty admitted to nothing. I kept asking her to come clean and she would glare at me and walk away. It made perfect sense that an older guy saw the opportunity and moved in, Patty being as desirable and horny as she was. I apparently wrote her a hateful letter, which I honestly can't remember doing, but I guess that was it. No more Patty and to this day I wish we had, just once, made wild love because I think if we had, Patty would be with me now and I might have had that career with the White Sox.

A year after the breakup I read in the newspaper that Patty had married. I drove all the way to the town where she and her husband were living, North Liberty, Indiana. I wanted to beg her to forgive me—to get the marriage annulled. I drove around that little town for hours hoping to see Patty. I had no idea where she lived. Finally, I just drove back to Bloomington. I had a date with Regan that night.

Things got worse when Regan's mother died just before college graduation. It was sudden and sad because her mother seemed perfectly healthy before she was found at home in a coma and a few days later she was dead. No cause was ever confirmed but the doctor guessed it was a brain aneurysm or tumor. Before that unanticipated and untimely ending I had the break-up with Regan all planned. I wrote her a letter explaining how letting Patty go was a terrible mistake and how I couldn't

40

stop thinking about her. It was a five-page letter but with a dead mother, how could I give it to Regan? I tore the letter into little pieces and threw them on the floor of my dorm room. A few months later, I gave Regan an engagement ring.

Back in the *Alibi*, I was trying to figure out why I never left Regan before the serious damage started and then out of the blue I remembered how Patty tried getting back with me before she married someone else. We went out one last time after that craziness got to me about her fucking for Shultz. It happened during a spring break and I remembered a black dress with shoulder straps. The dress was cut low enough to see the rise of perfect full freckled breasts—a nice tight fit—nothing like the pleated plaids and knee socks Regan wore. And I remember Patty's perfume— the scent of summer evenings, of proms, of firm silky skin on her perfect back and shoulders.

We went to the *Page Three* that night, a roadhouse with an atmosphere very different from the *Alibi*. Patty was getting looks from all the guys. The first slow-dance, we danced close and I had my hands on her perfect bare back. She put her left hand on the back of my neck the way Novak held Holden in that *Picnic* scene. They danced slow and sexy to *Moon-glow* and you knew she would be his forever. But as the night moved along and I held Patty close, a thought would not leave me alone: PATTY ISN'T LIKE REGAN PATTY ISNT LIKE REGAN PATTY ISN'T LIKE REGAN. It kept banging around in my head and by the time we got back to Patty's house I didn't even want to touch her, as if she disgusted me, or something. I could see that she was hurt and angry, but I didn't care. She said I owed her an apology for the letter because she wasn't fucking any- body and she knew that I loved her even though in that letter I said I never did. "What about the way you held me, tonight?" she said.

"What letter?" I said. Then I turned and walked to my car, a white Corvair Monza convertible. I climbed in without opening the door, started her up and drove away, top down, wind in my face. Just like that, I walked out on Patty.

Several years later, and a few weeks before I went to Vietnam in the winter of '64, Regan and I were married. I convinced myself that once married Regan would become more like Patty when it came to sex—more like CJ. Some Catholic girls were just late bloomers. That was the answer. But on our wedding night Regan begged me not to put my dick inside of her and the next night we had three hours of aimless foreplay in the dark and Regan started to cry when I tried to get on top of her limp naked body.

We came home early from Niagara Falls to see a doctor. Drove all the way to Indianapolis to see a specialist and after hearing our story and examining Regan, she said the problem was in Regan's head. She advised lots of lubricant. I knew I should have left her the night she washed her hands and cried. The last words I said to her before going to Vietnam for a year were "Get help" and she said, "I don't need help."

The US Army decorated me for bravery, a silver star for all the killing I did and a purple heart for a piece of shrapnel that punctured one of my lungs. But I still hated Regan when I returned home. I couldn't sleep in the same bed with her. She kept saying, "I don't need help" and I said, "Who cares."

Our next duty assignment was in Texas and my eyes and my dick started to wander. Leaving Regan was the only chance for me. I found a dream-girl named Tanner, a tall beautiful brunette with breasts like Patty's. We fell in love, had wild sex. I knocked her up and had the perfect opportunity to leave Regan. But Tanner went into labor early and the baby died at birth before I had a chance to divorce Regan and marry Tanner. I never saw that child, but the doctor told me she looked like something that wasn't human. "She had missing parts," he said.

I thought the missing parts had to do with how fucked up everything was. And there were darker thoughts, too, about that baby being a freak and dying because Regan had turned me into a freak and maybe even because of all the people I'd killed in Nam without remorse. Tanner tried to commit suicide and it was too much for me. I spoke to my CO and volunteered for another tour in Southeast Asia where the war would keep my mind from getting more fucked-up.

When Regan heard about Tanner and another tour in Nam she cried and several months later, before I shipped out she seduced me. The sex wasn't as good as what I imagined it would have been with Patty, or even as good as it was with Tanner but it excited me and it confused me.

The second tour in Vietnam was in a top-secret program. I worked with CIA spooks. It was dangerous, which was the whole idea. But Regan had confused me and now that conflicted state of mind became a distraction and one day I fucked up. I was supposed to kill a village elder, a known communist sympathizer with a great deal of local influence. The knife was in my hand to slit the old gook's throat as he slept. I crawled into his bamboo hut so quietly he never moved, but standing over him I heard a baby cry out in the night and hesitated because muddled thoughts about killing and Regan and babies were banging around in my head. The old man woke up, had a sawed-off shotgun tied under his cot because the Vietnamese knew about the night killings. He hardly moved but the damned thing somehow went off. It was aiming too low to kill me. It just destroyed my legs.

The guys who were with me killed the old man, his wife and children, even his grandchildren. They killed everybody in that village. Then they called in a chopper to evacuate me. While we waited they looked at what was left of my legs—ribbons of red and white hanging from my charred pants and they set the whole goddamned village on fire before the chopper arrived. I watched it burning as the helicopter lifted off.

Months later I was transferred from an Army hospital in Hawaii to a Texas VA hospital. Regan never came to see me in Hawaii but the first time she visited in the VA hospital she announced she was pregnant. She ignored my missing legs and when I tried to mention them she said, "Now, now, James, not to worry," and patted me on the head.

They fitted me with prosthetic legs and I learned to walk again. Regan gave birth to a baby girl who was beautiful and smiled at me the first time she saw my face. The next four years Regan worked as a teacher and I took care of our daughter (Regan named her Rhona).

No baseball for me. I was a permanent gimp. Violent thoughts banged around in my head day after day and once you've been violent, you worry you can be violent again. I saw a shrink who suggested I leave Regan for a while, "But what about my daughter," I said. He stared at me with empty eyes and then a smile that looked more like a grimace crossed his lips. "What's worse?" he asked.

I tried to explain it to Regan. "Everything happened so fast," I said. But she said, "I've suffered enough in this lifetime, Jimmy." She said, "Nobody is going to take one more thing away from me." But how could I ever look my daughter in the eye if I strangled her mother or broke her neck, or stabbed her over and over and over.

So I packed a small bag and left. Regan watched me and twirled hair. She never said, "Please don't go," or "I love you, Jimmy," or "Let's try to work this out." Not even an apology for being a selfish fucking ice-cube for all those years and then fucking up my head like that before I left on my second tour. No. She just sat there watching and twirling. And on her lap, doing the exact same kind of hair twirling was my daughter, the one who lived.

Regan took to hating me and that was when we did even more damage because Regan told Rhona that I didn't love her. She said I abandoned both of them and that if a dad loves his daughter he stays. In time Regan convinced her it would be easier if she just pretended her father was dead. "Why suffer?" Regan said.

Inside the *Alibi* headlights of passing cars on old Route 37 caused strips of light to run up the walls to the rafters and disappear. Odd ideas flopped in and out of my head like what if the place were still doing what it used to do—college kids coming to the *Alibi* for dance and drink—would there be hope? I gathered up a handful of paper fragments and let them slip, one by one, back to the floor, trying to figure out what hope I had in mind.

As the last paper shard drifted to the floor, I thought of Patty, that she's sixty now, and lives up in Idaho with her husband. I thought about Tanner, that I have no idea what became of her. My right hand reached for the knife, to close it and put it in my pocket, but my left hand was fumbling around and patting my pants, a kind of thoughtless movement at first, then more purposeful. Yes, I wanted my cell phone, wanted to call someone, dream dreams again, but I didn't have any numbers, well, except for my daughter, Rhona, the one who lived but refuses to speak with me. If I called her she'd just hang up and have her number changed again.

I missed the reunion. At Bloomington airport, I returned the rented car and noticed the airport beacon piercing the night sky, first green then white as it turned atop one of the hangers far across the airfield. I slept for several hours lying across four chairs in the passenger terminal. When I awoke I called Tom and thanked him for letting me visit. He said, "Nothing will ever be the same without CJ."

I didn't mention the *Alibi*. "Keep in touch," I said and flipped the cell-phone closed. Outside a terminal window the frost-covered plane that would return me to Seattle had arrived and the far off beacon on that hanger roof was still, its light no longer summoning travelers from the ice-blue of an Indiana dawn.

THE FAR END OF THE BEACH

...Every human is a miracle because we go on in spite of
knowing we will eventually
lose everything we love...

From the movie, *Little Children*

It was the summer of 1948. I was just standing there in two or three inches of water, sea-foam at the edges, and a stiff warm onshore breeze—Jacob Reiss Park in Brooklyn. My father said no one was in the water because of an undertow. The lifeguards had the red flags flying at every station up and down the beach and they'd blow the whistle and yell at anyone who went in further than ankle deep. I didn't know what an undertow was except that it didn't sound like a good thing.

"Hey kid, don't go in any further. I don't feel like getting wet today and your parents don't need to hear that you're lost at sea. The undertow is strong, kid. You'll drown." That's what the lifeguard with the white stuff on his nose said to me and it reminded me of a movie I had seen where something pulls a girl down into this deep pool somewhere in darkest Africa. It looked like such a small pond, but they never found her. The sea water was cool on my feet that hot July day, so I stayed in up to my ankles, and ran away from any big wave that rolled in after pounding in the surf like a thunder. Where does undertow come from and why do lifeguards put white stuff on their noses? You don't know this when you're eight years old.

Back then, we came to the beach on Sundays. We came with my parents' friends from Jersey City and Manhattan. We were from Weehawken, which was in New Jersey and famous for the Lincoln Tunnel, the Ferry, and the dual between Hamilton and Burr.

My parents were unusual. They often screamed at one another. When my mother screamed at my dad, she also punched him if he was close enough and then my dad punched walls and broke furniture. He picked up chairs and tables and smashed them down so they broke into pieces. When my dad broke furniture and my mother was screaming I sought shelter behind the sofa and if my bladder was full, I usually pissed in my pants.

The sofa was my choice because I never saw my dad pick that up and break it. Except for the sofa and the hutch, furniture did not last long in our house. I didn't fit behind or under the hutch. My parents did not seem fond of one another. Why did they get married in the first place? Weren't mothers and fathers supposed to be friends? I don't know where that idea came from—maybe from my best buddy Ed's folks. I never saw them scream or punch. Never saw any broken furniture at Ed's house or in any of my other friends' homes.

Sometimes my mother screamed at me. And sometimes she bled. She said the bleeding was from where I came out of her. She called it hemorrhaging and the word frightened me. When she hemorrhaged she also screamed and an ambulance would come and take her to the hospital.

Sometimes I told her I hated her and I did. It was the screaming and hemorrhaging. I'd bang my head against the wall when she bled and screamed. When she returned from the hospital I'd say I hated her just loud enough for her to hear it and she'd say she hated me, too. But whenever she said that she had a funny smile on her lips and I suspected she was kidding me even though I figured I must have done some serious damage when I came out of her. At the time, I had no idea what the hell I was doing inside of her, anyway.

Since none of my friends ever mentioned that their parents bled, screamed or broke furniture, this led me to conclude that my parents were unusual. Fortunately I did not dwell on this. Certain truths about life and love were unknown to me at this time. Two older sisters protected me from difficult fearful truths. They provided me with books about wonderful magical make-believe places where people were mostly happy.

So I'm standing there, ankle deep in the Atlantic and my oldest older sister comes along with her new husband and asks if I want to walk with them to get an ice cream cone. I love ice cream cones, particularly sugar cones with black raspberry, butter pecan, and mint chocolate chip. If given the opportunity a triple scoop cone with all three flavors will be my selection, but they only have one of my favorites at Jacob Reiss Park—the mint chocolate chip. I'm okay with this and the long walk in July heat to the ice cream stand. I like ice cream and my brother-in-law.

My parents like the far end of the beach. Less crowded is what they say. There are no concession stands at the far end of the beach, so it's about a mile walk to get to ice cream, which like the Atlantic Ocean, is cold. Besides, my brother-in-law says we can walk with our feet in the water. My brother-in-law is smart. He goes to college.

My oldest older sister is a nurse and her new husband was in the war. He fought in Germany, house to house. He was a platoon leader. He tells me stories if I ask. He carried what was called a burp gun—automatic forty-five caliber—he says it sounds like someone burping when it fired is why it is called a burp gun. He was wounded by shrapnel in the arm. He got a purple heart and a bronze star. He is still a reserve second lieutenant. I'm proud of him. I want to be like him.

I like the story of when his platoon sergeant was taking a shit in a doorway and a Nazi tank came around the corner and my brother-in-law told the sergeant they had to get the hell out of there. The sergeant pulled up his pants, shit and all. Still my brother-in-law got hit with a piece of shrapnel from a shell that tank fired, but his platoon knocked out that tank with a bazooka. A bazooka looks like a pipe and shoots a tank-destroying rocket-kind-of-thing.

My oldest older sister and her husband hug and kiss and laugh. It appears to me that, unlike my parents, they are happy. We hold hands, me in the middle, all the way to the ice cream stand.

What if they share fifty-one years together, then he dies of cancer and she becomes demented? She will say when she is becoming demented that she wishes she would have married the doctor who wanted her to run away with him just after she married my brother-in-law. What if she takes pictures of herself and gives them to me because she knows that she is disappearing. What if when my brother-in-law dies of cancer I'll be much older, and a physician, but there will be nothing I can do to save him or my oldest older sister? After my brother-in-law dies, that doctor she did not run away with may send my oldest older sister a locket. He may also send her kind letters and have a wife who doesn't die. My oldest older sister may not die, either. She will sit in a chair in an institution and talk to a stuffed cloth doll. And what if when I visit she will not know me? She will be dead, but not gone. I may look at the pictures from when she was alive for awhile, pictures of happy hours shared, but then I'll stop looking.

We walk the beach all the way to the ice cream concession. A triple scoop mint chocolate chip sugar cone is my choice. My brother-in-law pays the man. He gets the mint chocolate chip, too. My oldest older sister likes peach.

I call her my oldest older sister because my other older sister is not as old as my oldest older sister. This youngest older sister does not seem to like sitting around at the beach. She sings and plays the piano. She is very smart. Speaks three languages. Translates literature for a living, but would rather be an actress or a singer. She got a scholarship to Julliard for her piano playing but she didn't take it. Mother and Dad were very upset and then they were sad. Of course, Mother screamed and Dad broke a soup bowl against the kitchen wall. It had green pea soup with slices of red frankfurter in it so besides the crash of the bowl slamming into the wall it made a colorful mess. Nonetheless, my youngest older sister did not go to Julliard.

What if my youngest older sister never makes it in show business? What if she takes alcohol and valium and I never know if she found happiness because what if she decides that the rest of us, me, my oldest older sister, my brother-in-law and Mother and Dad all freak her out and she disowns us? Maybe she will stick to the disowning until she dies of cancer from smoking cigarettes. What if she dies when she is sixty and her husband whom I will never know has her cremated and spreads her ashes at Cape Cod? I will think she must have liked Cape Cod. What if after she disowned us she won the fight with alcohol and valium? And what if when I hear and think these things I will be an older well respected physician and professor of medicine, and still a warrior of sorts, but none of this will help my youngest older sister in any way?

So we are walking back down to the far end of the beach where Mom and Dad have the Indian blankets, the two yellow and green umbrellas, the very heavy green metal coolers, one filled with food and the other with iced tea, and where the wooden folding beach chairs with three shades of green, beige, and red striped cloth seats and backs sit under the umbrellas. Each time we come to Jacob Reiss Park we make a long hot portage carrying all of these essentials from the parking lot to the far end of the beach. We walk through tunnels where your voice echoes if you shout. My dad and I always shout, "Hey." I do my share of carrying to the far end of the beach, always glad it is not the far, far end of the beach because the walk is already long enough for me. Homosexual people go to the far, far end of the beach and mostly people who are not homosexual do not go there.

Sometimes the homosexual people put on little plays. When they do that, lots of the people who are not homosexual walk or run to the far, far end of the beach and watch, because the plays are funny. Homosexual men play both the girls and the guys in the play. When my dad sees homosexual men walking on the boardwalk toward the far, far end of the beach he climbs up over the railing and walks behind them swinging his hips and waving his arms with his hands in an odd wrist-dropped way. My dad drives a truck for a living. He quit school in the eighth grade. He wanted to fight in World War One but he caught typhoid fever and couldn't go.

I know what homosexual means because my mother tells me. She says it has to do with men and women who fall in love with other people who are the same sex as they are. She says they can't help it. She tells me this because I have a friend who may be like that. He plays with dolls. He wants to be the mother. He acts more like a little girl than a boy. I get into fights because of him. Everybody makes fun of him but my mother says I need to protect him because he is my friend. But my mother made him my friend, so she should have to protect him is what I think. I'm tough in certain ways. So I fight for my friend who wants to play house and be the mother. I fight and get bloody noses and then I wish he would like stickball or street hockey. Sometimes I wish that Mother hadn't made him my friend.

What if my friend who wants to play house and be the mother will learn to date girls in high school, but in college he will fall in love with a fellow? What if at forty-four he will have a fever and a rash and he will call me and ask for help because he will know I am a professor of medicine and a well respected physician? What if I send him to a famous infectious disease specialist but he will nonetheless die from AIDS in six short months? He will ask me once he recognizes that he is going to die what he can do. What if I will tell him he can die well and courageously and help educate other gay men so they do not contract AIDS? But what if he tells me that was not what he wanted to hear and I will not know what else to say to him even though I am a well respected physician and professor of medicine? What if nothing I can do will save him? And what if when he dies in the seclusion imposed by his mother who is ashamed of his homosexuality, I will cry on the inside for him and the torments of his life?

As we return from the ice cream concession and get closer to the far end of the beach, I see my father running toward me waving his arms. He is far away but may be making fun of the homosexuals. As we get closer I hear him screaming. He is screaming at me. There is a crowd around my mother and she is crying. She is screaming and crying worse than I can remember her screaming and crying ever before. As my father approaches I see that he may mean to do me harm. Hiding behind my brother-in-law who knocked out the Nazi tank seems like a good strategy.

My father, while screaming and crying, says my mother thought I was taken out to sea by undertow. Because of my history of stubbornness they thought I went in too far and the undertow got me. He says when my mother noticed I was no longer standing where I had been, ankle deep in the Atlantic, the lifeguards actually went out in there catamaran and rowed around and dove down trying to find my body. Then they told my mother that if the undertow got me I wouldn't be found for a long time or maybe never. So now she is screaming and sobbing and even a sympathetic crowd cannot comfort her.

My father keeps trying to get at me and I'm worried about what he intends to do once he gets those big hands on me. My father used to be a professional boxer. He might break my head. My brother-in-law and my oldest older sister keep saying it is their fault because they asked me to go with them for ice cream and my father says I should have told my mother I was going for ice cream and everyone is shouting and waving hands.

And then my mother notices me standing with my dad and my oldest older sister and my brother-in law and she runs over and hugs me and holds me and cries and says she loves me.

My dad quiets down when he sees my mother hugging me. Then he comes over and hugs me too, but he doesn't stop crying.

What if many years later, my dad will also cry after he has several strokes and can't think or speak in a manner others can understand? Perhaps I will sit next to his bed and rub his forehead and his hair with my hands and tell him that I love him and thank him for being a good father to me and then I will see the tears slowly make their way down his cheeks. I will be a respected physician when this happens, and still a warrior of sorts. I will also be a grateful son because my dad loved unconditionally. But neither respected physician, nor warrior will be able to save him from more strokes, eventual pneumonia and death.

And what if my mother outlives my father by five years but gets cancer and suffers? When she is suffering perhaps she will not scream. She will tell me not to cry for her because she had a wonderful life. "My life was a shining star," is what she may say. Then the pain will get much worse and she will cry out in the night and ask me to help her. I will be a respected physician when the pain gets much worse and being a respected physician is what she will have wanted me to be. I will adjust the morphine drip so she no longer cries out in pain before she dies quietly in her sleep. Perhaps this is why she wanted me to become a physician.

We went to Jacob Reiss Park on summer Sundays between 1947 and 1956. We usually stayed until everyone else left the beach and headed for home. My mother and the other women would sit on blankets in the gloaming, umbrellas closed, the men and children often taking one last swim in the Atlantic as long as there was no undertow. That particular day remains clear in my memory.

The water felt warmer as darkness came on. It has to do with the ambient air temperature in the evening when there is no sunshine. My mother and her friends were discussing life, things lost; children, adults, and other things that could be or had been taken away.

When the rest of us came out of the Atlantic and dried off, if there was drift wood, we'd build a fire and sit and think and smile in the warm firelight. Occasionally we'd toast marshmallows. This was when I began to learn the truth about loss. But maybe it isn't a good thing to learn at too young an age—that everything is eventually lost by everyone—that humans mostly find ways to hide this truth from themselves; they rarely come to terms with what they know—eventually, we lose everything that we love.

"Make sure it's out, and bury the ashes under plenty of sand," the beach patrol ranger would say if he saw the fire and drove over to the far end of the beach. Now and again there might be other firelight further up or down the beach, but always there were the lights of boats far out near the horizon like fireflies hovering over the black water. Back then how those boats found their way home in darkness or why they were out there in the night was unknown to me.

The night they thought I had drowned we did not build a fire or go into the water after dark. There was a big wind. The breakers were pounding and the smell of cold seawater was in that wind. Still, that night, we were the last to leave the beach. It was dark when we packed up and headed for the parking lot, carrying all of our beach things to put in the trunk of my dad's '36 LaSalle. As I balanced a folded umbrella on my shoulder and carried a rolled blanket under my arm I walked backwards all the way to the steps that led to the concrete walkway because I wanted one last look at those far-off lights on the horizon and wondered if I would be feeling anything had the undertow taken me out to sea. Or if those lights were visible from under the water. Do you feel things when you're dead, like the coldness of sea water? They're all gone now—family and friends who were there the day my mother thought her young son had died.

Years later, I will buy a sailboat. I will remember those lights on the horizon and learn to find my way home in darkness. Sometimes I will anchor off beaches in many different places and when darkness arrives, set the anchor and turn on the masthead light. The boat's halyards, driven by the night's wind rising, will beat a pleasing rhythm against the mast. That hymn of wind and halyards will bring magical memories. Sometimes I will share these nights with lovely young women who often wind up naked in my arms out on deck. And I will make love to them so they sing out like night seabirds, harmonizing with the hymn of wind and halyards.

Now and again, shortly after dark, firelight will appear at the far end of some beach, an orange-yellow far-off-twinkling like a star waiting for a wish.

A NEW MILLENNIUM

I'm driving south on Interstate 81, returning home from a business trip. It's January. The rain is pouring down. I'm in northern Virginia and I'm worried about freezing conditions. I see a small herd of Black Angus heifers walking along barbed wire, up a hill that has those three crosses on the top. They're a Bible belt thing—the crosses that is. And I'm thinking maybe Black Angus live an odd life, maybe they don't. Just then my cell phone rings.

It's my wife but at first I can't understand her. Her voice is all wobbly and the rain is noisy. Then I get it. She's crying—the words trying to get out between tears. My wife almost never cries. I remember one other time, when her aunt decided to tell her she wasn't her daddy's daughter. She cried on and off for a couple of months back then.

Right away I think something has happened to her, or maybe one of the kids. "Honey, what's the matter," I say.

"Ralf just killed the cat." She's barely able to get it out.

Ralf is our dog—a German Shepherd. He's usually sweet, but he's never liked the cat—the cat that showed up a couple of days before the new millennium. I was setting up for the fireworks display—putting the launchers in place for the airbursts I'd fire off in celebration at midnight, when this little cat appeared. She purred and meowed and rubbed up against my arms, but she was a mess—hair all tangled and matted, and she smelled awful.

Now I have to tell you, we live on a mountain in the middle of nowhere—no neighbors for miles. My wife saw the cat standing by me and she smiled. "I know that cat," she said, "I've seen her in the woods. I'll bet it was two or three months ago," and she sounded proud.

"She looks hungry," I said, and I don't know why we both thought it was a she. We didn't think she had claws, either, but she did. She just never showed them. And of course the dogs were barking at her—mostly, Ralf, who's four and frisky. Bodie, our other dog is a working Black Lab. He's old and he's seen a lot of dying. You could tell he only barked at the cat because when Ralf got started, he thought he was supposed to follow suit.

You should have seen that cat, no bigger than a half-year old kitten, stand up to those dogs. They were twenty times her size. She'd growl and hiss—I mean really growl, like a predator—a bobcat. She never backed off. She'd bat Ralf so fast and so hard on the nose that you could hear the contact—*thump*, and he'd back off and just look at her with his head cocked to one side in confusion or something like it. I only saw her run from him once, and that was so she could get under a chair and then stand her ground. So, I never worried about him getting her. She was too fast and too tough, and she wanted to be with us. That's what I thought. And I guess I thought Ralf wouldn't kill another creature. I don't know why.

We called her K.B. Millennium—Millie for short and the K.B. stood for 'kick butt'. We came up with some other names, too. My wife suggested 'Freedom', "like in the Kristofferson song," she said (she even sang the line: "*Freedom's just another word for nothing left to lose.*"). And our neighbor's five-year-old granddaughter wanted to call her Tabby, but we settled on Millie.

Millie had it rough, surviving in those woods with bears and coyotes. It was cold and I knew she wanted in the house because she'd try to follow me in, but we didn't need a house cat. So we agreed, if she wanted to, she could hang around outside. We fed her plenty and we gave her an old insulated cooler for shelter. She seemed content.

Then at the millennium party somebody was a mean drunk—tossed the little thing off the deck during the fireworks display. It's forty feet down from the deck to the first treetops on the mountain. I didn't see it happen—didn't know about it till the next morning because I was too busy with the fireworks. One of our other guests said Millie hissed and cried out in the air and then they heard breaking branches and more cat-sounds as she crashed somewhere down in the dark—yes, just a mean drunk. I might have stopped it if I had known.

She wasn't around on the First, so we thought she had died from the fall. I left on the business trip feeling badly. But she showed up again a day or so later. My wife called to tell me (long distance service is free on the cell phone). That's when my wife noticed Millie was pissing blood, so she took her to the vet who verified that Millie was a she, had claws, and serious internal injuries.

Now the rain is really pelting the car, and my wife is saying that Ralf got her. "Millie didn't even try to run," she says. "It was awful. He grabbed her and shook her—I yelled to make him let go. Then I wrapped her in a towel and held her." My wife is really sobbing now. "She was lying on my lap with her little paws crossed and she was shaking and blood was coming out of her mouth and she just gasped and died." My wife gets it all out in one breath.

"I'm so sorry, Darling," I say. And I wish I could say something more meaningful, but with the rain and all, I'm having a time. "I guess the dog didn't know any better," I say. Then there's a lot of static and we lose our connection.

Now I'm terribly sad, too, thinking about that little cat—such a hard life—and I can't see with all the rain. But it gets worse because this idea hits me out of nowhere—*she only had a borrowed life. Borrowed things have to be returned*, I'm thinking. And I don't know why, but *something borrowed and something blue* runs through my head. Maybe that's all she had—nothing old or new. Then a memory of our little daughter who died ten or fifteen minutes after she was born oozes out. She didn't come with all her parts and when the doctor saw what she looked like, he tossed her onto the stainless steel sink in the delivery room. I suppose he meant well, but I remember her gasps and her trembling—then she was still (and I remember how normal her tiny hands and feet looked). My wife didn't see—she was doped up. But I did. And then there was my sister who died from hate and alcohol—no old and no new in her life, only defeat—*maybe like Black Angus*. These thoughts are flying by in forms resembling jagged edged shadow shards.

The phone rings again. "I don't know what happened," I say.

My wife apologizes for the tears.

"No, it's okay, it's very sad," I say, "It's like Millie had a borrowed life." And I hear the tears get started on the other end, again. I have to pull off the road for a few minutes. I can't believe we're so sad over a stray cat.

It stops raining and I can just make out the sun because it's going down behind the mountains. And then I'm thinking, *maybe Millie let Ralf get her—wanted him to, like the hate and alcohol got to my sister.* The line is quiet. "Honey, are you there?" I say.

"I'm still here," she says.

I start to drive, again. Before I know it, I'm doing eighty and we're both crying. What's left of the sun creates odd long shadows and the static starts again.

"I wish I could have been there for you," I say. I'm shouting into the phone.

"I know," she says.

The phone goes dead and I have this really bad feeling because it's getting dark fast, and colder, too. Then I see a herd of dairy cattle—black and white ones. They're all huddled together in a barnyard. I figure they're waiting to be let into the barn—to be milked and fed and for some reason this makes me feel better. After awhile I slow down, and start watching road signs, looking for a place to eat and rest. And I'm hoping they'll have a payphone so I can call my wife back. I'm thinking, *Maybe we'll do better with a payphone,* maybe not.

Then it hits me, I've never allowed myself to grieve. I had plenty of opportunity with my dead daughter and my dead parents and my dead sisters and my dead best friends. I have to pull over again. Fortunately, there's a Rest Area.

DOES JESUS SAVE THE LIVING?

He learned that drills and pretending to kill were different from the actual killing—the practice didn't prepare you for the violence, the blood, the smell of death. Echo Team, Special Warfare—he was the commander, Michael Warren, First Lieutenant. Back in the sixties and seventies the teams worked in many places—South America, the Middle East, and of course, Vietnam. Special Warfare teams were air-mobile and missions were at the request of the President, spoken of only in 'safe' rooms. This is what Michael told me.

A week before Christmas in '72, Echo team was sent to Vietnam. There were five members, Michael Warren an Army Ranger, John Davidson a Navy Frogman, Peter Romano a Marine Corps Sniper, Tom Fish, another Frogman, and Andrew Rangal, another Ranger. The team had been in Vietnam before. Missions were officially labeled as information gathering or sometimes, they didn't even exist. But they always involved killing. On this trip, a helicopter which Michael called a Huey, was taking them to a remote location in the jungle just above the South's border with North Vietnam. It wasn't a place the enemy would expect Americans to be. What's more, Michael did not look like a typical American. His mother was Chinese.

The Huey flew low and fast to handicap would-be shooters and to muffle its wind-hammering turbine-driven approach. A 26-year-old Michael sits in the open doorway looking down on the wet gray mist that blankets the jungle canopy—my home. Water vapor condenses on his skin, soaks the black bandana tied around his head. Droplets fall to his hands and sparkle momentarily with starlight before they evaporate in the wind. The humidity is one hundred percent and the ambient temperature ninety-nine degrees. They're wearing black—look like Vietcong from a distance. Their faces are covered with black grease and except for stars in the heavens and gray mist below, the night is also black.

Peter is shouting so Michael can hear him over the wind and the engine. He's second in command. Michael said when Peter was nervous he asked pointless questions—he was from California.

"Lieutenant, how much farther?"

Michael leans close to Peter. "We've been flying about an hour," he says loud enough to be heard. "Maybe another thirty or forty minutes—relax, for christsake."

There's a village twenty kilometers northeast of where the Huey is taking them. It is near Vinh Tuy. At the time it is the staging area for a Vietcong unit recently arrived from farther North. The leader of that unit is a grandson of Ho Chi Minh. The CIA uncovered this piece of intelligence and the mission is to kill the young man, wipe out his VC unit, and destroy all their supplies. It is believed that such an act will give the enemy a taste of the heavy price for continuing to fuck with the United States. These were Michael's words. And with the Navy and Air Force again bombing the North, Lieutenant Warren suspects this mission is an effort to add pressure for peace. Killing for peace—which I do not understand.

"Lieutenant, go over this map with me," Peter says because he is wound tight.

"What the hell is eating you?" Michael says. "We'll talk on the ground."

"Okay, okay Lieutenant Warren, Sir," Peter says. "Sorry. Very sorry." He turns his back—folds his arms across his chest.

Lt Warren leans close again. "Put the fucking map back in your fatigue pocket before it blows out the door," he says. The most elite warriors get irritable before a mission but all will change when boots contact the jungle floor.

John, Andrew, and Tom sleep. It's been a long three days of travel from the tangled jungles of Honduras along the Patuca River where, far from prying eyes, they practiced drills and rehearsed for the mission in a place constructed to look like the village near Vinh Tuy.

The Huey's blades begin to thump hard against air leaving spiral ribbons of condensation like flying ghosts, behind the tip of each rotor blade as the craft slows and descends closer to the mist below. The team slips into pack harnesses. There is no conversation, no wondering about starlight. The helicopter hovers five feet above the tree-tops that poke through the clouds of mist in the vague glow of first light. There is a brightening eastern horizon and patchy, now pale, mist over the trees as these seemingly invincible Americans slide down ropes to the ground, sixty feet below. Once on the ground they listen in gauzy darkness to the Huey's thumping blades growing feint—then gone. They listen for movement other than their own.

These teams work alone. They're inserted and extracted, equipped with what they need—nothing more or less. The United States believes these quiet deadly missions have powerful psychological impact on a primitive and superstitious enemy and I suppose my people were primitive and superstitious. Because deniability is essential, they carry no radio. Assistance is out of the question, rescue, self-defeating. They are on their own until extraction.

Echo Team goes through the usual drill, moving off in one direction, then, carefully doubling back to be sure they're not detected. They head in the opposite direction from the village for about thirty minutes—another precaution. When they are certain no one is following, they rest. They are in the enemy's jungle. They've been here before—trip-wires, mines, snares, poisoned spikes, venomous snakes, tigers, centipedes the length of your foot—every square inch of ground a potential death trap.

Michael is uneasy, but he knows how to hide his emotions. He said he learned this from his mother. He moves well in the rhythm of jungle sounds. Quiet blending is part of his genetics. Dressed in black they seem to be what they are not. Michael watches the man in front and behind, places feet carefully, reluctantly. The process is consuming—hunter and hunted. Watch the tiger hunt, it looks similar.

Periodically they stop for a second or two and in their silence they listen like the predator cat, and by midday they're more than halfway to the village. They slip off packs, drink water, eat freeze-dried food. Now, it's time to review the plan.

"John and I are on the north side of the village. First we set up clay-mores and then, once Andrew and Tom start the attack...," Peter is going over his and John's job, "we lay down killing fire. If we have to break and run for the phony LZ, we set off the claymores—draw the gooks chasing us into a kill-zone. And if we get a shot at that grandson gook bastard, we take it. He will be the team leader. His name is Ho Sin Chi. Then we cover your ass, Lieutenant, while you blow up any stores you find in the village. We meet right here," he points to a spot on the map Michael has spread out on the ground. "Finally, we hump another five clicks along this trail—his finger works the dotted dark line on the map—and the Huey picks us up."

Michael says, "Remember the Huey will be there at 1400. Don't miss your ride." And he doesn't seem to mind the word 'gook;' even uses it himself from time to time.

John wipes sweat and insects from his face. The insects stick to the black grease. John has an easy way about him. He's from Minnesota. "Kill a Commie for Christ," he says, and then he makes the peace sign and grins.

"Peace on you too," Michael says. They laugh.

John and Peter take up the sentry positions. Andrew and Tom crawl next to their young leader. "Okay, show and tell time," Michael says because you need a lot of coolness before death and killing.

Andrew does the talking. "We move to the east of the village, so the sun is rising behind us—plenty of glare. Start shooting as soon as the sun rises above the tree line, just enough to blind anyone trying to shoot back. Killing fire—accurate. Our first responsibility is to kill that gook, Ho Sin Chi. When they set up to fire back at us, Peter and John lay down heavy automatic fire. That's when we use the white phosphorus grenades. If it gets too hot, we draw them toward us by laying red smoke, like we're marking a landing zone for a chopper and when they sucker for that, we use the claymores. And, oh yeah, we'll try not to kill any innocents." Andrew laughs.

"Who's innocent?" Tom says, but he doesn't laugh.

"What about egress and pick up?" Michael says.

Andrew knows the drill by heart—indicates the right map locations—knows the exact times.

If you didn't know better you might think Tom didn't give a shit, but it's just his way, detached and cynical. He is point—goes first because he hears, smells, sees better than any of them. He detects the smallest movement, the faintest odor, the softest sound. He can hear the sun rising is how Michael described it. Tom is mostly quiet. Comes from Kansas. When the team is on the move, he leads, Peter follows, then John, then my Lieutenant, and finally, Andrew. Andrew, the country boy, friendly and open. He has a wonderful smile. He comes from Texas. Women want to mother him. Andrew watches the team's back.

"Okay, we've got an hour," Michael says. "Take a break because we won't stop again until we're there." He lies on his back, resting his head on his hands which touch earth that's soft and warm and smells like mushrooms and ammonia. He looks beyond the canopy at small patches of blue, through holes forming in the mist clouds and thinks about the team, about minimizing risk—about who is innocent. He said for an instant he saw his mother's gentle dark eyes. Perhaps she's thinking of him. But this is not a place for mothers.

Michael first heard of Special Warfare when he saw the pin on the recruiter's uniform—an eagle and a snake. If you made the grade, you were the top of the food chain. You got to wear the pin over your heart, the raised golden eagle clutching the silver snake in its talons. That's what the recruiter, who had lost a leg in combat, told him and it made him think of knights, the Round Table. He was twenty-one. Needed a quest. It all got started in college—Brown University, because he was an Easterner, a dreamer, full of himself and full of a place called Camelot, which I have heard about.

But maybe it got started before that. His father fought in the Pacific during the war against Japan and afterward married Michael's mother who was from Formosa. They met in Virginia at a garden party—she was part of the Nationalist Chinese diplomatic mission to the United States, a very bright and gentle woman. After the war, his father was stationed at the Pentagon, an American Military Attaché to the Nationalist Chinese Government. His father told Michael it was difficult back then, because of her eyes and long black hair, the cold war, other things. His mother did not speak of such things, but Michael saw their truth in her composed eyes.

He remembered the red neon sign that hung on the front of the Baptist Mission across from the recruiter's office in Providence where he went to sign up for his new adventure. That sign said '*Jesus Saves*' and it flickered on and off and spit white sparks with a snapping, cracking sound.

He was commissioned after graduation from Brown, then spent many months in training: Infantry School, Airborne School, Ranger School, Survival School, martial arts, demolitions, weaponry, small unit tactics, psychological operations and after all of this, a final six months in Special Warfare School. He survived and became one of those elite warriors, received his Eagle and Snake two years after graduation from college.

His parents attended all the ceremonies but seemed distressed. He thought they would be pleased, realizing that he finally became the knight he always thought he was. Now, after so many missions he understood their concern, but for him it was too late. For him there was responsibility and duty.

Michael concentrates on the mission, trying to ignore sweat running down his face as softly as his mother's loving fingers—forcing out of his consciousness that red neon sign and his mother's eyes. His responsibility was the west side of the village. Dense jungle and higher ground border the west side—a good place for VC sentries he thinks. He'll kill them. He carries a 9mm German automatic with a silencer, a piano-wire garrote, a knife; all made for the quiet delivery of death. It is also his job to protect the team in the event of what Tom calls a goat fuck. And if Andrew and Tom don't get Ho Sin Chi, Michael must do this job, himself. Finally, he will go into the village and blow up weapons and ammunition. He carries fragmentation grenades for this purpose. Michael will look for useful information and speak to the villagers. His CO always says Michael's eyes are an advantage on such missions. Michael has his mother's eyes. He is equipped for this job, but doesn't dwell like Peter because if he dwells, he loses the edge. Ice cold is how my Michael survives.

The remainder of the journey to the objective is hot and wet, every moment filled with attacking insects and the tension of the hunt but otherwise uneventful. First light comes at 0530 and Michael is already on the west side of the village. He finds no sentries, no booby-traps, nothing. As planned, they weren't expected and he's thinking this is good. He's almost in position when he sees movement in shadows a few feet in front of him—a small boy; maybe he's five or six at most. He has dark sad eyes that look at the black bandana, the pistol, the long knife. The young eyes speak fear and Michael holds a finger to his mouth—*keep quiet* he says in perfect Vietnamese. He tries to tell the boy he's a friend—a *brother*—that he won't hurt him, but the boy is too frightened and foolish. He turns and runs toward the village shouting, "A killer. A killer." Michael Warren takes careful aim at the small back with his silenced German 9mm, but he doesn't shoot.

There is shouting and Michael moves in closer to get a look. Vietcong are all over the village. The team counted thirty the night before when they silently scouted. They even identified Ho Sin Chi. Now the boy-child runs up to him and points in Michael's direction. Ho Sin Chi shouts orders.

"Weapons! Weapons!" he says and some VC run to a small shack—come out with a rocket launcher, AK 47s. While they're handing out weapons, Ho Sin Chi gathers women and children into a semicircle—places them between him and where the boy pointed. One young girl is screaming, resisting. She is twelve and has an infant in her arms. Ho Sin Chi grabs her by the hair and spins her around. He shoots her in the chest and the AK 47 bullet makes a cloud of blood-mist as it bores through the two bodies, which fall to earth in a heap, smoking like fresh dung. The shot echoes in the silence of early morning only slightly muffled by the mist. The infant's legs stick out from under the older girl's body. They quiver, stop, quiver again. Then still.

Ten or so VC including Ho Sin Chi move in Michael's direction using the rest of the women and children as a shield. The women have fear in their eyes, the little ones whimper. The boy-child kneels beside the two dead bodies, patting them; trying to awaken them, but Michael does not see this because the other women and children block his view. Some VC shove and slap the women and children to keep them moving. Others crouch behind mud walls and wooden crates in the village, AK 47s at the ready. What could have been a quick and efficient ambush is turning into a disaster.

Michael is talking to himself. "Goat fuck," he says. "Convert fear to useful energy," he says. It's what he's been taught and he is reminding himself as sweat crawls down his grease-darkened face. He stands up, in plain view of the approaching VC. It is the foolish boy's doing that makes this act of courage and potential sacrifice necessary.

"Ho Sin Chi," he shouts in Vietnamese, "What are you doing on my land? This is my jungle. These peasants pay me to protect them!"

Ho Sin Chi stops walking and stares at Michael. He is confused by the sound of his name and the sudden appearance out of the tall grass of this seemingly Asian warlord in VC clothing. He hesitates, but does not speak. Michael continues to walk slowly toward him, his hands shaking in this dance with death, but Ho Sin Chi cannot see this because Michael keeps them behind his back. He walks with a slow swagger as if confident and proud. But he is holding a grenade—the pin already pulled. When he is within forty feet of Ho Sin Chi he stops and speaks again. His Vietnamese is perfect.

"Hey! Are you unable to speak? Are you stupid? My men have you surrounded, waiting for my command," he says.

The VC open fire, shooting from the hip and their bullets hiss over Michael's head. Their weapons crack and thump. He feels the violence of bullets only millimeters away from his head and chest. He falls backward as if hit. The shooting stops. The VC talk to one another—excited choppy phrases. They're still confused—probably not combat seasoned is what Michael is thinking. His ears are ringing from the muzzle blast of AK 47s, the air is sharp with the smell of gun powder.

The VC open fire again as if to reassure themselves, but Michael has crawled from his original position in the tall grass and again, no bullet strikes him. Now, there is silence, broken only by the occasional whimper of a child—the tearful whisper of an old woman.

A few more moments pass and like a hunted tiger in tall grass, Michael is still. He watches. He sees that now all the VC have moved out into the open—makes out some of their words, "....dumb warlord....target practice...." The VC laugh and Ho Sin Chi says, "Some killer."

Michael sees the boy walking toward Ho Sin Chi, a gentle morning breeze raises the child's straight black hair. The boy is carrying an AK 47 that is almost as long as he is tall. Ho Sin Chi looks toward the boy. Tells him to hurry so he can see a dead killer. The VC slowly move forward to find the dead warlord's body in the tall grass.

Michael sees that the sun is rising above the tree line into a blinding white blaze and right on schedule Andrew and Tom begin to lay down killing fire. All the VC are out in the open—not combat seasoned. Then Peter and John start shooting but Michael can see their muzzle flashes. The sun's glare is not hiding them. White phosphorous grenades explode and VC are screaming and dying. So are villagers. Ho Sin Chi trades with one of his men, his AK for a rocket launcher. He is still hiding behind women and children. Many of the women and children are already shot by bullets meant for him. Some are burned from the white phosphorous grenades. Michael cannot see the boy.

Ho Sin aims the rocket launcher at Peter and John. Michael said he knew they would die. He holds the fragmentation grenade in his hand, ready for use. His fingers seem welded to it because the pin is out, but instinct pries them free and he throws the grenade at Ho Sin Chi with deadly accuracy. There is that crunching sound of killer fragments tearing through air and anything else in their path. Ho Sin's body falls to earth, missing half a head and spurting blood like a broken pipe. But as he falls, the rocket launcher fires, perhaps a reflex in his dead finger closed down on the trigger. The rocket strikes the ground a few feet from him and another explosion kills many more women and children and wounds others so they lay bleeding and screaming in a great circle of body parts and blood. Michael sees the boy, his hair still blowing in the gunpowder scented breeze. He is on the ground and he is still.

In minutes all the VC are dead. So are many villagers. Michael enters the village, blows up weapons, destroys food, ammo. Villagers stand around and stare at him. They flinch and duck when the grenades explode down in the holes or inside huts where these things have been stored. He takes bloody papers and maps from what remains of Ho Sin Chi. A group of villagers, mostly women and children, are tending to the dead. The men have been taken north for training to fight these American killers. They point at Michael Warren, show him a severed leg, a hand, an arm and they say, why? Why? "You are not from here," they say. "Why do you kill us? Why do you care? We have enough trouble," they say.

Michael Warren does not speak to them. His eyes stop for a moment on the boy, whose body is in the arms of one of the women.

Later, Peter will say, "What a great distraction you created. You have more balls than brains."

Michael will shrug.

Then Peter will say the gooks killed their own women and children. He will say, "Ho Sin Chi fragged kids and gook bitches with that rocket."

"God damn them," Andrew says.

John seems to agree, his head nodding. But Tom doesn't say anything, doesn't nod or even look toward Michael. Tom sees and hears everything.

"We have to catch our ride," Michael tells them.

After that mission they fought some other fights together and they were good, these elite American warriors. But eventually the team was broken up to spread their experience around. Michael was moved to Intelligence, and promoted to captain and then to major. Always his eyes helped him to go where others could not go. Peter and John were killed in action in '73. Tom remains MIA. Some years ago on a rainy morning Andrew walked out to his garage and started the car, but he didn't open the garage door. The local newspaper said it was an accident. They said he had a wonderful smile.

Only Michael Warren was left. Years later he came across that Eagle and Snake pin in a box in his attic. It was all tarnished. And there were pictures of him as a kid in the same box—black and white pictures from when he dreamed of knights and roundtables and that place called Camelot. In the pictures he had gentle dark eyes and straight black hair like his mother's and like mine. As he sat looking at the pin and the pictures he tried to remember *their* faces—Tom, Andrew, Peter and John— but nothing appeared not even Andrew's smile.

He sat there, in the attic on the chair that had belonged to his mother. Some of the furniture from their house was in his attic. He shared it with his sister after their parents passed. He had more room to store it because he never married. It wasn't that he didn't think about marriage. There had been some lovely young women who seemed interested in him. But he never felt he had the right to be a father. He had lost it somewhere—maybe in that village near Vinh Tuy.

He sat on the chair in his attic and he looked into the mirror of his father's old dresser. He tried to see his mother's eyes, but they were gone he thought, the softness and the brightness. He wiped the pin on his shirt but the tarnish held. He placed it back in the old cigar box with the combat ribbons and the crossed rifles he had worn on his collar before he was transferred to Army Intelligence. He served out his twenty years and retired, as his father had done before him. After, he opened a small shop in Mount Royal. He sold children's books. In the winter the shop was cold and he wore an old yellow sweater that had belonged to his father.

In the mirror's reflection, a knight of sorts, head bowed, hair straight and gray, kind Asian eyes—wise even, but tired, sad. He placed the box in a drawer, descended the stairs and made us a pot of tea.

I know this man very well. He came back to Vietnam and found me. He brought me home to America. He said it was the least he could do for me. He became my father. I remember the day he came to my village as a warrior. It was my fault that my sisters died and all of those other people. He said he was a friend and told me to be quiet, but I was a frightened little fool. Michael was brave. I am glad he came back for me. That was over twenty-five years ago. Now, I'm almost thirty-five and still this kind man loves me like a son. He will leave all of his earthly possessions to me, as well as the love he has given me. Nonetheless, I'm confused by innocence—trying to understand who is innocent and who is not. Nothing seems to help me understand. I want to ask Michael, but I'm uneasy about it.

CAPITAL G GOD

Failing to fetch me at first keep encouraged
Missing me one place search another
I stop somewhere waiting for you.
                              Walt Whitman, Song of Myself

Hanna Johansen was ninety-four. She told her son to call a cab and get
her to the hospital. Hanna did not feel well for the first time in her life.

"Mom, maybe you're overreacting," he said because she had never
been sick. He was sixty-three and could not recall one instance when his
mother had not been in perfect health.

"Nope," she said. "Call a cab, Sonny."

He hated being called Sonny, but Hanna assigned the name when
he was an infant because she had named her two children, both sons,
Frank. Their father, Frank Johansen, was a fisherman. His boat, *Chance
Encounter,* disappeared on a fishing trip when Sonny was under a year
old. Hanna never removed the wedding ring she said she and Frank
bought when they learned she was pregnant. They went to City Hall in
Baltimore to get a license, and were married a few weeks later by a Justice
of the Peace. Hanna also loved Frank Sinatra and didn't want one son or

the other to think she favored him because she named him after her husband or her idol, so she just decided to name them both Frank. Sonny's older brother was Frank B. Johansen, named after his father, and Sonny, Frank S. Johansen, was named, according to Hanna, after Sinatra. She called his older brother Buddy.

Buddy lived in San Francisco. He was an artist. Painted watercolors of the Northern California coast and sold them in various boutiques that catered to tourists. He made a living. He was gay. He'd had the same partner for the past twenty years. He also had AIDS but it was the slow killer kind. Buddy looked as healthy as Sonny, who had nothing wrong with him except that he was a widower because his wife died suddenly of a rare heart ailment a week after he married her. She was only thirty at the time, Sonny was forty. And so he moved back in with his mother, who complained bitterly about the invasion of her privacy.

Hanna had a live-in lover at the time. She was seventy-one. Her lover, Harry Turnipseed was a fifty-two year old who had been with the Barnum and Bailey Circus for his entire life. He'd traveled the world with the circus. Knew how to do everything from setting tents to being a catcher for the high-wire act, to training ponies for the lady in the passion pink tutu who rode on their backs around and around while the circus band played a medley from the Unfinished Symphony, American Patrol, and The Monkey Chased the Weasel. Harry had affairs with many lovely circus ladies and seemed generally happy until he came down with Rheumatoid Arthritis one summer while the circus was in Baltimore, which is where Hanna and Sonny lived.

Hanna met Harry one Sunday morning when she was volunteering at the local Red Cross shelter down near the harbor. She cooked there every Sunday because she liked meeting merchant sailors and vagabonds of other types who came to the port on trains or boats and then had a run of bad luck and had to stay for a time until some position opened up in the rail yards or on a freighter or tramp steamer.

Harry used the name Butch Dollar as his circus name. He said it was given to him by some of the folks who found him on the circus grounds back in 1932 under the bleachers in the Big Top. They weren't sure just how old he was but figured maybe a year or so. He was raised by this circus family, home schooled, and taught the ropes, so to speak. Part of the story was true, but Harry, known as Butch, actually was delivered to a ring master by his mother, a Baltimore hooker, who had become pregnant during a torrid affair with a sailor. Her name was Flora Turnipseed. There was something about Harry that Hanna found irresistible (he looked like Sinatra), so she took him home.

Hanna wasn't much on mulling over decisions. Once an idea formed she either liked it or she didn't. If she did, she acted on the spot. Sonny had just gotten married and was going to live in Philly. Buddy was off in San Francisco and so it was time, Hanna figured, to get on with her life. This Butch Dollar fellow wouldn't be able to work anymore, had a modest pension, and he needed some help. Besides he was handsome and Hanna was missing the presence and intimacy of a man in her life. She was horny and didn't mind admitting it.

"Look, fella," she'd said to Butch Dollar, "I have a big old house and it's pretty much empty. I'd like to take care of you if you'll take care of me." She winked at him.

Well Butch damn near choked on his roast chicken and tears were running down his cheeks.

"What the hell is so funny about that?" Hanna said.

"I've never been propositioned in quite that way," Butch said. Then he told Hanna his life story.

"Well. I kind of like Harry Turnipseed better than Butch Dollar," she said after hearing the somewhat abridged version of his life. "Butch Dollar has a ring I don't think I can warm up to. Harry Turnipseed is unique and endearing. Well grounded as far as I'm concerned." And she laughed at her own humor.

And that was that. Harry it would be, for all of their years together. Harry and Hanna had twenty-one happy years before the Rheumatoid Arthritis disfigured Harry's body so badly he couldn't find a comfortable position and found it hard to breathe. Hanna had been saving up all the painkillers the doctors prescribed for Harry over the years that he hadn't taken. Mostly he hadn't taken them because Hanna used other means to relieve his pain. Harry loved oral sex, and as long as he reciprocated, she was always willing to have him ejaculate in her mouth. "Two or three blow jobs a day keep the doctor away," is what Harry told her in private, choking and teary eyed from his silly laugh.

But Hanna suspected the arthritis would eventually win out and when Harry turned seventy-three, the pain was unrelenting. He couldn't find any comfortable position. It was at this point that Hanna and Harry had the talk.

"Well, my dear sweet Harry, you've made the last twenty-one years a joy for me."

"Thank you, Hanna. It's been a great ride for me, as well."

"I think we need to end your suffering," she said.

"I agree. Do you have a gun so I can shoot myself," Harry asked.

"Too messy," Hanna said. "But I did save several hundred pain pills. I'll bet we can get you off to a better place with grace and ease," she added.

"Won't all those pills make me throw up?"

"If we grind them up and give them to you in some apple sauce and chocolate pudding, maybe your stomach won't complain at all."

Harry loved apple sauce and Hanna's homemade chocolate pudding. She spent several hours making the pudding and they always had several jars of apple sauce in the refrig. By noon on the day Harry passed, Hanna had spoon fed him fifty of those pain pills all ground up and served in pudding or apple sauce.

"Ya know Sugar Lips, the idea though sound, is scary," Harry said as he ate his final desert.

"I'll miss your calling me Sugar Lips," Hanna said.

"Sugar Lips, Sugar Lips, Sugar Lips," Harry added.

"I'm sure it is scary. I often wonder what dead is like. I mean I suspect it's nothing, Kind of the way it was before we're born. But who can be sure. That's what makes it scary—the-who-can- be-sure part."

"Ya mean the uncertainty of it?"

"Yes, probably worse than uncertainty because who wants to end—cease to exist. What the hell is that about? Now I'm conscious and then I'm nothing."

"Well, ya certainly have been something," Harry said.

"Such as?"

"Well, there's your life and your good deeds and your shit deeds, and in your case your boys, and then there is your matter—all those molecules containing atoms containing all of those other little things with funny names."

"Well that makes sense. Except I can feel a lot of those little molecules right now, but once I'm dead, my guess is they're on their own."

Harry tried to move and let out a long soft painful groan. "Come on girl, let's get on with it."

It took about 45 minutes to get most of it down and shortly after, Harry was fast asleep, never to awaken again. About halfway through the first bowl of pudding they said their goodbyes because Harry could tell he was headed for the light, as he would say euphemistically, because he didn't think there could be a god or a God in such a cruel world as he had observed in his life. "Life is what it is," he would say. "No god or capital 'G' God needed." His last words to Hanna were, "See ya around Kiddo." And she said, "Yep, see you around dear man."

"It ain't so bad," he said with his last exhale.

The following morning, Hanna called his doctor, and said Harry hadn't awakened. She said she thought he was dead. The doctor came to the house and thought Harry had died because he could no longer breathe. The arthritis had molded him into a form that didn't allow for much chest wall movement, including breathing out and breathing in. He made the death pronouncement and called the coroner. And that was that.

Hanna had his corpse cremated. Then she hired a plane and a pilot. It was an old Stearman, the kind with an upper and a lower wing. She asked the pilot to fly her out over the Atlantic. She carried his ashes with her in a small box and when she saw blue water and a hazy horizon she asked the pilot to turn the plane upside down. As the Stearman rolled over she let loose Harry's ashes and said, "Gone but not forgotten, Turnipseed—you were a fine fellow."

Hanna was ninety-two when Harry died. Sonny noted a minor loss of energy, but still his mother went to the Red Cross Shelter's kitchen at least once a week and prepared some nutritious meals. She had gone to that Shelter every week for as long as Sonny could remember. And when Sonny moved back into his mother's house, he did find it uncomfortable that his mother had a lover who was so much younger than she. Sonny tried to stay clear of the two of them and set up a small suite for himself on the second floor of his mother's large Baltimore Victorian home. He always knocked on the front door as he opened it and announced he was home before climbing the spiral staircase to the second floor. Sometimes Harry or his mother would acknowledge his return, but sometimes his "It's just me, Sonny," would get no response except silence. Sonny made his own dinners in the small kitchen he had added to his second floor suite. Occasionally, before he left for work in the morning, Hanna would invite him to dinner.

He actually enjoyed the dinner conversations with his mother and her lover. Harry was charming and had many great stories to tell from all those circus years. He also could spin some philosophical perspective on life from his stories, which added to the interesting conversation. Sonny particularly enjoyed the debates about God versus no God. Sonny was a believer in something, although he wasn't sure, exactly, what it might be. In his mind it made no sense that the cosmos would be here by some accident of matter and energy. His mother was on Harry's side, mostly. She saw no need to add 'little g god' or 'capital G God' to the mix. Life was what it was, nothing else made sense to her.

She was a fan of Darwin and of science, which may be why Sonny had earned his doctorate in astro-physics and been on the faculty of Johns Hopkins for years. But Hanna always thought Sonny was searching for something out there in the cosmos—something that would answer the questions he had about life and death and the passing of time.

"When it's over Sonny, it's over," she'd say. "Life is filled with enough choices and possibilities, we don't need more of anything really, especially once we're gone. And time, it's just an illusion."

"But what if there is more? What if we need to be searching for more?" Sonny would ask.

"How much do we know about the here and the now? Do we know everything?" Hanna would say. "Do we have to prove that 'capital G God' is not a bologna sandwich?"

"Mother, don't trivialize."

"I'm not, Sonny, you are. Looking for something you will never find. Just keep learning all the wonders of the here and the now. Isn't quantum mechanics enough of a hunt for you? Won't that kind of searching give up some important answers?"

Hanna was very well read and quite an intellectual. And Harry was a game participant. So supper together was never dull. Harry was more of a pragmatist than Hanna. "If ya live in the circus, ya see the side of life that proves there's no big G or little g god. There's some smiles and a lot of suffering. Folks have expectations that are silly. Not only is the 'god' idea silly, it's down right foolish. What kind of god would order up all of this suffering?"

"Suppose it's for atonement?" Sonny said.

"Atonement for what? Are you proposing a vengeful god and that original sin shit? Really? So I'm supposed to buy into the idea that the force that's responsible for the stars and planets and galaxies, and evolution of matter into life and so much more we don't know, is also a mean simple minded vengeful bastard? Really? Come on Sonny. It just can't be. You and all the rest of the big G godders, you're just wishful thinking because ya can't deal with endings," Harry had said. "Ya all just can't deal with the truth so ya make up the bullshit."

"Maybe you're right Harry," Sonny said after thinking about Harry's perspective. "But I can't even imagine just ending. It's creepy."

"Well then don't try. Just live each day and get all ya can out of it."

Sonny missed Harry once he was gone. Had no idea his mother and Harry had engineered his ending and Hanna played her cards close—which is why she hadn't mentioned the occasional pain in her chest and jaw, when she walked from the bus stop to the Red Cross Shelter. It started before Harry left, and she knew what it was and hoped it would end her soon. At ninety-four she figured she'd had enough. She was tired.

Once they arrived in the Baltimore City ER, Hanna was unconscious. One of the ENT's announced, "94 year old female probably having an MI accompanied by LVF and what look like some runs of electrical/mechanical dissociation."

Sonny got the message. The ER physician said he should have a seat and they would call him once the team completed an evaluation on his mother. Sonny felt some distress, even though 94 was 94. He wondered if he should pray for his mother, although he would admit he really wasn't certain who or what might be listening. He closed his eyes and tried to free his mind, which is hard to do when a person is very smart. It's like there are just too many underpinnings to let the mind loose.

In his head, he began to form the words and phrases, Whomever might be listening, please make this easy for my mother. She's been a very good person. If there is something more than this life, please offer her the best available. She'll probably say she doesn't need it, but don't listen. She can use a nice comfortable rest." But then Sonny recognized that a simple quiet ending might be a very comfortable finale as well—an endless rest. Maybe nothing more was just fine. But the idea definitely made him uncomfortable. He thought of Harry. Was he just gone as well? What about himself? What does it feel like to be gone—gone from your own consciousness? It's like disappearing; even the very idea of it is most uncomfortable.

Hanna wasn't herself at the moment. Wires and tubes were attached and inserted and all the data was pointing to total cardiac failure due to an old worn out heart muscle—one that had been well used. Of the little blood there was being pumped out with each lingering beat, just enough was getting up her carotids and vertebral arteries to deliver molecules of oxygen sufficient for one more conscious thought. Her eyes opened and although she wasn't clear about where she was, she did have an idea about what was going on, and just enough mitochondrial fuel to formulate a few words. Sonny stuck his head into the cubical because he thought he heard his mother stir or maybe he got some kind of odd feeling. He was looking at her cyanotic face, and he knew what that blue tint meant. He was about to shout for the doctor but didn't because he saw his mother's purplish-blue lips begin to move.

Hanna seemed to be speaking to no one in particular. "I think I'm dying," she said.

"Now, now," Sonny said.

"How long will this take?" she said, and that ended it. Hanna was no more.

Sonny was about to make the funeral arrangements. A local and well respected funeral parlor kept a liaison person in the Baltimore City ER. This was done as a convenience, they said, but it also accounted for over thirty percent of their business. 'In a time of need, it's the least we can do' is what it said on the business card carried and offered by the liaison. On this day, a Thursday, the liaison was Vincent Fiori. He was a pleasant enough fellow, short and plump, but he had a soft concerned kindness about him and sincerity was clearly visible on his face. Sonny was reading the words on the card Vincent had handed him when one of the ER nurses touched him softly on the shoulder and said she had found a note in his mother's pocket. She handed it to Sonny along with a small plastic bag containing the neatly folded clothing his mother had been wearing, including her usual black orthopedic shoes, and a smaller plastic bag with the wedding ring she said she couldn't get off her finger ever since Sonny could remember.

"How did you get that ring off her finger?" Sonny asked.

"It just slid right off," the nurse said.

"But she always said she couldn't get it off." Sonny was upset at the apparent discrepancy. He hated discrepancies.

"Maybe she lost some weight," the nurse said.

"We can put the ring back on her finger if you'd like to bury it with her," Vincent said.

"You'd better read the note," the nurse said, gesturing to the still folded piece of paper in Sonny's hand.

Sonny looked at the folded paper and recognized it as coming from one of the note pads Hanna kept setting in various places around the house, each accompanied by a number 2 lead pencil so if something important came to mind she could write it down before she forgot it. She found the pads at a yard sale. They had Disney characters in bright colors up in the left hand corner. She'd been doing the note pad thing since she turned eighty-three. There were over a dozen pads in various rooms, including several in Sonny's second floor suite. He had noticed, a few years back, that many of the pads were yellowing in the corners, from age and exposure. Nonetheless, the piece of paper in his hand which had Mickey Mouse in the upper left hand corner, was neatly folded in quarters and had three words written on one exposed surface—'Somebody Read This.'

He carefully unfolded the paper and noted the following written inside. *If you are reading this I no longer exist. If you knew me, please share your memories so I won't be too soon forgotten. Also, please cremate my corpse and put what's left someplace where my molecules will be available for reuse. Maybe someplace where birds nest and breed. That's it, and thank you, Hanna Johansen, once female human*

After Sonny read the letter, he kept hearing his mother's words, *"Just keep learning all the wonders of the here and the now."* And that's when his brother Buddy, whom he hadn't seen or spoken to in years popped into his head. Sonny didn't really know him anymore—almost like he didn't exist. He saw a payphone booth in the hospital lobby and decided to call his brother and share the news of their mother's death. He had a pocket full of quarters and dimes used to ride on the buses that were his means of transportation. He wondered if this was an example of meaningful chance.

WHITE DAISIES

For Honey and Lonnie

My father said after the death of his parents and his four siblings that going to Philadelphia would never be the same. I was too young to understand what it was that would never be the same. I enjoyed family excursions to Philly. Long rides on old Route One beside the Erie Lakawanna line, where more often than not I'd get to hear and feel the blowing hissing thundering rumble of a great steam locomotive pulling a mile of freight cars, hoppers, and tank-cars between Jersey City and Philadelphia. The smoking black monster slowly overtook my dad's black '36 Oldsmobile coupe and there it was, slightly above us on the railroad right-of-way that paralleled Route One for much of the trip. My dad might have been doing thirty-five or forty, but the locomotive was doing forty-five or fifty so the pass was slow and delicious to my eight-year-old eyes and ears. Usually more than one hundred cars would slowly pass us by and I'd look at the names printed on them—names from all over North America —Canadian Pacific, New York Central, Norfolk and Western, Norfolk and Southern, Baltimore and Ohio, Virginia Southern, Union Pacific, Erie Lakawanna. I'd look for livestock in the cattle cars or if the tankers had a skull and crossed bones designating what my mother said was something deadly. It was an odd feeling, looking up at that enormous tank car so close and filled with something deadly. As steam gave way to electricity and then to diesel power the great steam monsters disappeared from those tracks, but still, I loved trains. They were my first hint of life's wonders.

On the way to Philly, somewhere between Jersey City and Linden, I usually got car-sick and vomited. This was the only bad part of those trips. Mother brought damp cloths and napkins. Dad hated it when I vomited because it made the car smell. I tried not to, but mostly it happened, that dizzy hot feeling and then the pressure in my chest, the fitful salivating and finally the heaves from stomach to mouth followed by whatever might be chewed up and digesting down there.

But for some reason, when my older sister, Annie, came along on the trip, it was different—no vomiting. She sat in the back with me and we'd sing songs or look for letters in alphabetical order on license plates. She'd rub my head or scratch my back. We'd marvel together at the locomotives and count the wheels,

"It's a 4-4-2," or "It's a 4-10-2!" The bigger the engine, the greater the excitement and the longer the train. I got to know a lot about railroad trains because of Annie. "See the brass bell on top of the engine." Annie would point at it. "See how the engine is round above the wheels. That's the water tank." She told me about the coal-fire heating the water into steam and the steam driving the wheel pistons. To my eight year old mind, steam engines where the greatest thing in the world. And trains, from engine to caboose were made of so many cars, varied in appearance and function, but moving with a purpose—all connected. My young mind suspected there was something to this.

Annie was a pretty girl and she always smelled like flowers. Her perfume remained the same for as long as I can remember—*White Daisies*. She called me Silly-Willy back then, and when I grew up it changed to just Willy. No one else called me that, ever, although my middle name was William.

In '47 Annie finished college and joined the Navy. By then my father's mother had died along with one of his brothers. The car sickness was infrequent and although I missed my sister, those deaths didn't faze me much. I loved seeing the steam locomotives and the food my father's sister Rosemary prepared—Hungarian and German. Mostly I loved her dumplings and potato pancakes. And when I had to go look at my grandmother's dead blue-gray body in a black dress with hands folded on her abdomen looking like someone had switched her real face with one made of clay, it didn't mean much to me at nine, except for the sound of water dripping under the casket.

I looked up at my sister, thinking Grandma may have sprung some sort of a leak.

"It's the ice melting," Annie said.

"What Ice?" I asked.

"The ice necessary to keep Grandma's body from smelling."

"I noticed that smell all the time," I said. "That's why I didn't like her to hug me."

Annie smiled but I didn't understand. My father's mother had always smelled unpleasant. She was very old when I knew her, already well into her eighties. She was older than my father's father by almost ten years. It had been an arranged marriage.

She came from Hungary with a significant dowry that got my grandfather started in the flower business.

Seeing my father's mother dead on ice wasn't much of a thing, at the time. At least she didn't smell any more and all I could focus on was the Hungarian goulash Aunt Rosemary was preparing for the occasion of Grandma's death. In those days, wakes were still done at home, the corpse laid out in the parlor on that bed of ice with the catch pan underneath and a nice burgundy or dark green cloth draped to the floor so you couldn't see the ice or the pan. The smell of goulash from the kitchen and flowers in the parlor was all I could focus on. It didn't occur to me for some years that flowers at funerals might also be there to hide the smell of a corpse in early decay. It also didn't occur to me at nine, that death was more important than it seemed.

Decay is an interesting natural phenomenon. It's meant to do good—bring things back to some reusable form. It's nature being wise. It's the way the cosmos perpetuates itself. Everything decays back to something more useful. We have certain words for it because there is something unpleasant associated with the idea of decay like the initial image of the process; the odor, appearance, or even dangerous radiation when something unstable like Uranium or Plutonium decays. We say rot, or shit, or corruption. We say radiation poisoning or we say spoilage, decomposition or senescence. Decay never sounds like a good thing. It rarely, if ever, evokes pleasant images.

Years later my wife and I lived in the Maine North Woods for a few years and the nights could be so very still—well, except for the crickets, cicada, and the tree frogs—and the old barred owl perched on a tree limb waiting for her meal. A young rabbit, gentle, meek, soft, crept along the ground, instinct telling him to be very cautious. But he was out in the dark—his first year of existence—not cautious enough. Rabbits are generally silent. But when the she-owl dove from her limb, making no sound, and her talons clutched him and her sharp hooked beak tore his skin from his muscle and disemboweled him while he lived the experience, he cried out in the darkness—a long high-pitched tone. It causes you to awaken and the cicada, crickets and tree frogs to go dead silent. It isn't a nice sound and you implore the owl to kill the poor rabbit. "For christs sake just kill it," I'd whisper. "Just get it over with." And the cry would diminish and turn to a soft whimper and then be done. For that small meek creature, death was terrifying and painful, unexpected and premature. It can happen that way to any living thing.

When Annie visited us and heard this crying out for the first time, I explained to her just what it was. She cried for several hours. She said her tears were for all the rabbits that died that way.

My sister studied Russian in college and her work with the Navy had something to do with her command of that language. She never spoke much about her work and after five or six years of Naval service she met a Norwegian sea captain while her ship was in dry-dock for repairs sustained in a North Sea storm. Otto Kiefersson was his name and he told me years later that he was taken by my sister's bearing, intelligence, and good looks. Word was they were going to get married. I heard mother tell her friends.

Otto owned his own small freighter named *New Munich*—five thousand five hundred tons, One hundred seventy-five meters long. He was handsome and wealthy. I thought everyone should have been happy but they weren't. Annie sent pictures of Otto and the ship. I remember the straight white stack with the red stripe painted near the top and the light gray hull with *New Munich* in white at the stern. Annie said it was rare for a sea captain to own his own ship but Otto, who loved the sea, was from old Norwegian money—shipbuilders. Dad said he looked German and his name, Otto, was German, and his ship was named after a German city. My dad fought against the Germans in World War Two. He still had issues. I think this may have been difficult for Annie—my father's mistrust.

But then it looked like Otto was out of the picture for reasons unknown to me, and there was a new guy in Annie's life, Robert McCord, a Canadian physician. He wasn't as handsome as Otto Kiefersson, or as rich but we got to see lots of pictures of him and Annie holding hands and hugging. They met in London while Annie was stationed there in '52. Again there was talk of marriage but then McCord returned to his home in Nova Scotia and it turned out he was married, even had some kids. I figured Annie must have been very sad and maybe angry but she never spoke of it. I heard Mother telling Dad about Annie and Robert and how she was seeing Otto again. Apparently Otto really loved my sister. And once Dad had Dr. McCord to be pissed at, Otto seemed to gain in status, German or not.

Years later I learned that Annie and Robert kept in touch over time, letters came to Annie at first in London and even after she married

Otto Kiefersson, they reached her on the *New Munich* in Singapore, Le Havre, New York, wherever mail caught up with the *New Munich*. Annie told Otto that Robert was a good friend and so the McCord family and Kiefersson family became good friends. Robert and his wife visited the freighter and took short trips or just visited while it was in port for a week or so in some unusual city.

Then Robert's wife died giving birth to their fifth child. Annie went to the funeral but Otto couldn't leave the ship. After the funeral Annie helped Robert out with the new baby for a few months until he found a nanny. Annie stopped home before joining Otto on *New Munich* in Suez. During that short visit in 1961, I saw in my sister's eyes that something was calling her to Robert, perhaps a voice she could not answer because of her promises to Otto. Nonetheless, I saw sadness in my sister's eyes, a soft far-off sorrow.

We never discussed it. I wanted to talk about it. I was in college and felt pretty good about my developing understanding of life and love. But Annie never brought the subject up and I didn't think it was my place to do so. Annie didn't like to discuss controversial issues or anything sad. I remember being in a pet shop with Annie and my daughter Sophie Anne, when she was very young. There were rabbits in a cage and Sophie Anne asked if rabbits made any noise. "Not to my knowledge," Annie told her.

Otto sold the freighter after a time, I think it was in 1999 or 2000 and they moved into a house in Orient, New York. By this time, the girls were grown and off living their own lives. I never finished college because I decided to make furniture for a living in an old barn next to my comfortable farmhouse in Mendham, New Jersey. I'd found my little pocket of happiness shaping wood into lovely tables and chairs and fine cabinets. I shared many memorable moments in that house with my wife and daughters. But now the girls were off on their own and it was just Sophie, me, and the collie.

After they sold *New Munich* and moved to Orient, once a year my wife and I would pack the collie, Creamsicle, into our '74 Ford station-wagon and head for Orient to visit Otto and my sister, and once a year they'd come and stay with us, usually around Christmas.

They never had kids, which was one of Annie's sorrows, I think. It was the way she always looked at my girls, made clothes for them and wanted them to visit for the summers, even after they had families of their own. And they did. The girls loved their Aunt Annie and as they got older Uncle Otto didn't scare them so much, either.

In fact, when my two daughters were 14 and 17, back in 1979 Uncle Otto invited them to spend an entire summer sailing on *New Munich*. The ship was carrying a cargo of exotic Asian spices to Copenhagen from Calcutta. Uncle Otto even paid for their flight from New York to Calcutta where they boarded the ship for the trip through the Bay of Bengal, the Indian Ocean, around the Cape and all the way up to the North Sea. It was just after that voyage that Otto had his first heart attack. He always joked that my girls were too much for him. He said if he had had children with Annie, he'd certainly have died young.

But there was some honesty to his joking because Otto never wanted kids. He was a work-oriented man. He loved Annie, but he loved the sea and his ship just as much. Maybe that's what was missing for Annie, never raising her own children and having to share Otto with the Sea. Life on the freighter for Annie and Otto went on for another twenty years after that summer when my girls sailed halfway around the world with them. But by then Otto was almost seventy and wearing down. He'd had several more heart attacks and his doctors and the maritime authorities all felt it was no longer wise for him to be a sea captain. So, they settled into the lovely Cape Cod cottage out on Long Island and it wasn't too many years later that Annie began to act strangely. She was sixty-five when it started, about three years after our mother died.

She'd called me almost every day at the lunch hour, when she knew I'd be taking a break from my shop.

"How are those lovely girls of yours?" she'd ask. "When will you be visiting again?"

I'd tell her about the latest news from New York and San Francisco, which is where the girls lived, now, Sophie Anne (named after her mother and favorite Aunt) was an architect with a West Coast firm, and Beth, the oldest, had two kids of her own, boys, and was an attorney in Manhattan. Nonetheless, my sister spoke of them as if they were still 14 and 17 and living at home—as if time somehow stopped back when they spent that summer aboard their uncle's ship.

"My little nieces love this place we've bought," she'd say. "There are plenty of handsome young men out here in the summer," even though the girls had never been there.

"You know Sophie Anne," I'd say, "She'll come see you as soon as she has a free moment." And it was true because Sophie Anne really enjoyed her aunt and uncle and their stories of faraway places and adventures at sea, like the unexpected typhoon they survived one September in the South Pacific.

Sophie Anne was not married, put career first and loved to travel. We sometimes said she was like her name-sake aunt, but she wasn't because my sister always wanted a life more like the one I lived or more like the one Beth was living, raising those boys of hers in Manhattan and going to Broadway shows and the Metropolitan Opera, the Zoo, walks in Central Park on Sundays. Sophie Anne walked a path different from both of her namesakes.

So when Annie would call at lunch and ask about her nieces, her voice would get wobbly and sometimes there were tears. I'd ask if she was okay.

"Sure Willy," she'd say, "If I were any better, I couldn't stand it." And she'd laugh.

But I knew she wasn't right. I felt the sadness over the phone-lines all the way from Orient to Mendham. And what I felt became a reality when Annie decided to make a trip out to San Francisco to visit Sophie Anne.

She and Otto decided to make a road trip adventure of it. Otto bought a new Mercedes coupe just for the drive. Annie called regularly as they made their way west. She used payphones. One Sunday in mid-afternoon the phone rang in an unusual way. It was an operator in Idaho.

"Will you accept a collect call from Annie Kiefersson?" the voice asked.

"Of course," I said.

"Hi, Willy," she said. "How are you?"

"You must be getting close," I said.

"No, we're in Idaho. We decided to go the northern route and drive down through Oregon."

"How's the trip goings so far," I asked.

"Oh, not so good," Annie said, "Otto's gone."

My wife flew out to Idaho to get her. Otto's passing seemed to take with it Annie's hold on the here and the now.

"Willy, I feel strange. Nothing is the same. Nothing will ever be the same. I think my memory has turned dark grey," she said.

I didn't really understand what she meant until she arrived in Mendham. But, I could see then, that she'd forgotten most of who she was and who she had been. She forgot that for years she acted like she loved all of us. Now she slowly turned angry and hateful. It started on the drive back when she said she never loved Otto and that I was a son-of-a bitch for having the life she had wanted. "Why did you have those girls? They should have been mine. You two have always been happy," she said to Sophie, "and I have not."

My wife drove Annie, the Mercedes, and Otto's ashes back from Idaho. Annie had him cremated out there. "It saved time and space," she said in a harsh manner and my wife was surprised because this didn't sound like Annie.

And when they got back to Mendham she spoke equally harshly of our parents. She cried for hours at a time. When she didn't have my wife confused with our mother, Annie would sit beside her and want to be held like a sad frightened child. And the look I had always loved in my sister's eyes, a bridge that lovingly connected the past and the present—that look disappeared. Over the months following Otto's unexpected demise my sister's eyes became cold and empty. They reminded me of the eyes of a horse I had once watched die, or the light on the front of those old steam engines when it wasn't turned on—cold and empty.

My wife Sophie always lived up to her name. She was patient and kind with Annie, even when Annie thought Sophie was her mother, when Annie cursed her for making her go into the Navy, for allowing our father to dictate her actions and choices. I tried to remind Annie that this really wasn't how it was, but when she began to drift around in time, she didn't want to hear anything except what she believed had happened in her now dark grey state of mind.

The doctors said it was a kind of depression, perhaps even a post-traumatic stress phenomenon. Apparently Annie hadn't been happy on board *New Munich* for all those years. And it seemed she really was in love with her Canadian friend from so long ago. She hadn't seen Robert McCord for years, but she spoke of him as if they were still lovers and she was planning to go to him and help raise his five children. I tried to remind her that those children were all grown up, now, and she scowled at me. "What would you know about love?" she said.

We had to sell the house out in Orient, and the Mercedes. Annie forgot how to drive and she couldn't live by herself because she suffered episodes of blank-mindedness when she would stop and look around as if lost in time and space. She'd look at me or Sophie as if we were strangers.

"What the hell are you doing on my ship? She'd say.

"You're not on the *New Munich* any more, Annie. This is your brother's house in Mendham," Sophie said.

"Who the hell is Annie, you bitch. I don't know any Annie, but I know you. You killed my husband."

It was hard for us, but not as hard as it was for Annie when she'd experience a brief moment of insight and perfect recall. Then she'd cry. She'd look at me and say, "I'm going blank." Or she'd say, "I'd rather be dead than forget who you are, Willy." And then she'd cry—soft wet tired sobs like she had when she'd heard that rabbit crying out in the night so many years before.

Annie didn't die. She lived on for several years and became meaner as her brain decayed. She suffered those moments of reckoning along with her decay for only a short time. Then she didn't know who she was or who we were, not even her nieces, and I saw it happen right there in my sister's eyes. Those same eyes whose brightness lighted my view of our shared past; those time-bridges that connected me to our now dead parents, my youth, and so many distant happy moments, like recalling all the cars in a mile long freight from engine to caboose. That light in her eyes faded. She became only an aging body. Her love, her memory, dimmed and then was gone, like a candle snuffed by an imperceptible evening breeze.

We kept her with us and eventually she became so ornery and combative she required sedation that left her unable to help herself in any way. Annie was a hundred and seventy pound mass of flesh that Sophie and I couldn't move to bed or chair or bathroom. We got a hospital bed and put it in what had been our TV room, took turns cleaning her piss and shit and when she stopped swallowing food we really didn't mind.

She slept away the hours for almost a month. We didn't bother her except that we did read to her and sing to her and we kept a fresh bunch of cut flowers beside her bed, always with some white daisies if we could find them. She'd open her mouth from time to time like a little hungry bird, but all she wanted was water which we offered her at first through a straw, but then with a dropper, recording the number of drops and the time in a book we kept next to her bed as if it mattered in some important way.

We were unclear about our feelings, Sophie and I. Did we want her to live or to die? I don't think we knew for sure. There were moments when the idea of her being gone made me come undone. In the privacy of my workshop my eyes would swell from salty tears. Speech wasn't possible because my voice was so wobbly. This coming undone would contain me until I remembered she was already gone. Annie had already told me of her fear and sorrow over what had become of her—her living decay, her profound senescence. I couldn't imagine her wanting to live if she had the choice. She would prefer death.

The thought occurred to me that it might mean something to Annie if we could get some advice from Robert McCord. After all, not only had he loved her, but he was a physician. Sophie didn't like the idea. She felt it would just make another person sad—ruin sweet memories.

I found his name in a registry of Canadian physicians. It said he was semi-retired, gave an address but no telephone number. A note on lined yellow paper—the kind lawyers like to use—just wouldn't come together:

Dear Doctor McCord,

I'm writing to you on behalf of my sister, Annie Kiefersson. She's become demented and I thought you might be able to help....

No matter how the words were formulated on that yellow legal paper, they never sounded sensible. What could Robert McCord do for Annie? She wouldn't know who he was even if he visited. Or would she? Perhaps his presence would shake her into some kind of miraculous recovery. Love might bring Annie back. I smiled at the thought, so foolishly hopeful and romantic. Sophie was right and this recognition began the hardest part of my sister's decay process for us—for me—the part where we accepted her ending but had to wait it out.

For months water was all we could get into her. She went from her 170 pound plump self to a tiny skeletal body that couldn't have weighed more than sixty or seventy pounds. Water in, water out. We changed her diapers frequently so she wouldn't get any rashes and we turned her from one side to the other so her skin wouldn't come off, but as she got thinner and thinner it did anyway. She developed smelly ulcers on her buttocks—three of them. We washed them out with peroxide every time we changed her diapers. It made little difference. Whatever was causing green puss to form kept causing it, along with a smell that resembled rotting food. Annie was in an accelerated phase of decomposition.

Sophie and I were close to despondent—figured we were failing in our duties to Annie even though we knew there was no way to prevent what was happening to her. But then it hit us. Nature was doing what had to be done. The decay needed to accelerate. That was the way it had to end.

Sophie Anne and Beth were staying away because they didn't like the feeling they got when they looked at their aunt in her hospital bed in what had been our TV room. Sophie Anne came once and Beth twice and that was it. Neither of her nieces visited Mendham and since we couldn't leave Annie unattended, only Sophie visited the girls from time to time. Beth was a train ride and a taxi away. Sophie Anne was another story. But Sophie did fly out to see her once during Annie's long bed-bound stay with us in Mendham.

Our girls said their aunt was gone and there was no point in visiting if Annie didn't know they were there. They both said the same thing; that they wanted to remember her when she was Aunt Annie not as something in physical and mental decay, her emaciated smelly body setting silent and motionless in the bed.

By this time Beth's sons were old enough to think for themselves and they had a slightly different perspective. The boys were five and eight. They'd come with their mother, on one of her visits to see Aunt Annie. This was before Beth knew what to expect. But now, having seen and smelled Annie, the boys had a kind of fascination with such a life-form. They'd never seen anything like it except for a dog carcass they'd stumbled upon in Central Park. The dog had apparently crawled into some bushes to die. The boys were chasing a ball when they found the carcass half eaten by insects and vermin. Beth explained natures way to them because the sight and smell were distressing.

"He was probably a fine friend to someone," she said. "But then he got old and just found a place to curl up and die. Now his carcass is providing food to other living things and that food will help new life happen," she explained.

Jacob, the youngest of my grandsons asked if the dead animal would make any new puppies because the boys had recently been given a Golden Retriever pup by their parents. Beth, thinking fast, suggested that a fox feeding on the dead carcass was pregnant and would be having a litter of pups very soon.

"Are there foxes in the Park?" my oldest grandson asked. His name is Adam. Beth said there were, even though she wasn't sure. She said they had poetic license to be there in the park. It was at this point in the discussion that Jacob asked why Grandma and Grandpa didn't put Aunt Annie's carcass out someplace to feed some animals and make puppies. He thought this would make his Aunt much happier then being smelly in a bed.

That night Beth called to share the story with us. Sophie and I smiled when we heard it but later that evening when my head was resting on a pillow and I was trying to stop thinking about Annie's terrible circumstances, the idea began to come together.

Was there any point in watering Annie? I read a book about death and dignity and it spoke of the withdrawal of food and water. Annie was already without food. According to the book, it was the water we were giving her that was prolonging her suffering and death. So we talked, all of us, the girls and Sophie and I. We decided to stop the water. It was Sophie Anne who suggested we plant a bed of white daisies in memory of Annie. "They will grow like weeds, but they're so simply pretty," Sophie Anne told us.

Annie has been gone now for more years than I care to remember. It only took eight days without the water. We had her body cremated and put the ashes into the new flowerbed of white daisies beside my barn. The boys, Jacob and Adam, loved coming in every spring to see Aunt Annie's flowers—the ones her ashes nurtured each year—white daisies that gave each spring and summer something special to anticipate. How many would there be? Would insect cross-pollination result in any color variations? Over the years, rare color variations did appear, but always the white daisies were there to remind us through many generations of our family about a life that was my sister Annie.

Sophie joined Annie a few years ago, and I'm coming up on my day. I work at accepting this without distress, but there always is an edge to it. My daughter Beth and her husband Joe moved out to the farm when Sophie died. I can't make furniture anymore, but Joe took over the work and I still do some varnishing and an occasional French rubbing to finish a piece. Sophie Anne moved to Paris soon after her mother died. She never married or had a child but she seems happy and visits the farm a few times each year.

That little daisy bed is almost half an acre, now—the whole south side of the barn for as far as you can see out the one window in the varnishing room. Beth's boys are men and they bring their wives and children to see this field of flowers. It takes very little work to keep it bright and fresh and pleasing to the eye. It's because it was a wise decision is what they tell their kids, this family bed of white daisies.

"Perhaps we'll all be lucky when our turn to end comes," Beth says to her grandchildren. "Perhaps we'll all become white daisies."

"Couldn't we become anything that feeds in that bed of flowers?" one of my great grandsons asks. He'd heard something crying out there the other night, and I told him about the owls and the rabbits. He looked sad and maybe even a little frightened, so at first I regretted telling him the truth.

"What would you like to become when your turn comes?" Beth asks her grandson. His name is William, after me.

"I'm not sure," he says, "maybe an owl, but I have a long time to figure it out, right?"

"Yes, William, a very long time to figure it out," someone says.

And I'm thinking it's better to deal with rabbits and owls then to make up foolish stories to avoid what's really going on.

Thoughts fill my head as my old hands apply a rich deep-toned French rub to finish the surface of a new table my son-in-law has made from one of my old plans. The white daisies visible through that large varnishing room window are dancing in a south breeze—the scent of alcohol and wood stain filling me with newness and memories. I'm thinking that after all this living, I finally understand my father's perspective of Philadelphia. From one day to the next, nothing can ever be the same. Perhaps it's a gift—newness and memories.

NOTES

NOTES

NOTES

NOTES

NOTES

NOTES

NOTES

NOTES

NOTES

NOTES

NOTES